ALL WAS LOST

Steven Maxwell is a PhD Creative Writing candidate and winner of the prestigious PhD Research Scholarship at Lancaster University. He lives in Wirral.

ALL WAS LOST

STEVEN MAXWELL

PUSHKIN
VERTIGO

Pushkin Press
71–75 Shelton Street
London WC2H 9JQ

1 3 5 7 9 8 6 4 2

ISBN 13: 978-1-78227-765-1

Designed and typeset by Tetragon, London
Printed and bound by CPI Group (UK) Ltd, Croydon, CRO 4YY

www.pushkinpress.com

Her rash hand in evil hour
Forth reaching to the fruit, she plucked, she ate:
Earth felt the wound, and Nature from her seat
Sighing through all her works gave signs of woe,
That all was lost.

MILTON, Paradise Lost

67

The detectives looked through the glass. The glass was one-way and beyond was a purpose-built chamber. The chamber's walls were concrete block fitted with ringbolts and against the far wall lay an iron-frame bed, thin mattress wrapped in plastic, headboard hung with manacles. Gazing down at what lay piled beside the bed on the poured concrete floor was the cold glass eye of a wall-mounted camera.

'What are we talking here?' Lynch said.

They were standing in the viewing room, a dark and narrow space that ran the length of the chamber, and maybe out of reverence for the dead or owing to the oppressive dimensions of the room, both men whispered when they spoke.

'Communication breakdown,' Carlin said. 'Transaction failure.'

Male and female. Some barely adults. A death-camp pile yoked together by their necks with collars and chains. Their hands and feet manacled. At least three of them had fresh purple scars hacking across the sides of their torsos. All had track-marked arms. All had been branded. All had been shot in the head. The blood under them flowing off into the trench drains had dried brown and begun to crack at the edges.

'No sale, kill the product,' Lynch said.

'Don't call them that. Just because they were treated like meat doesn't mean we talk about them like meat.'

'I know. Sorry.' Lynch gestured to the small metal desk beside them where a high-end laptop linked to the chamber's camera had been shot through its keyboard. 'Wonder if we can pull anything off that.'

'We'll see.' Carlin opened the steel door that led upstairs and looked back at Lynch, waiting for him to follow. 'Let's go.'

Lynch didn't move. He stood staring through his reflection in the glass at the murdered who lay callously exhibited in the dead fluorescent glare. One young woman naked from the waist down, sweater ridden up exposing the thin smile of a fresh caesarean scar. He guessed he was no more than five years older than her. His fists whitened.

'Lynch.'

He came to and followed Carlin out of that bleak cubbyhole and up the concrete steps to the hallway where polished oak boards creaked under their shoes. Below brass picture lights, framed paintings of foxhunts hung from the burgundy walls of the hallway. A hooded forensic scientist in white coveralls approached carrying a clear plastic bag containing an old Nikon F camera and several 35mm film canisters.

'These were found under the console table,' she said.

'Outside the living room?' Carlin pointed down the hallway. 'Right there?'

'Yep. Maybe nothing.'

'Maybe something.'

In the doorway of the green-painted living room, they looked anew on the carnage before them. Several men dead among scattered pistols and rifles and shell casings. Sound suppressors had been fixed to most of the guns. Some had their eyes open and looked as if they were about to talk, mouths frozen in speech. Two wore dark suits and Kevlar-lined leather gloves, white shirts blood-soaked. One of these men supine on the chesterfield couch still gripping a pistol, gut-shot, his entire midsection darkly drenched. The other on his stomach across the rosewood coffee table, the back of his head blown out, bits of skull and brain strewn about him. Curled under the table was a man wearing a black Adidas tracksuit who'd taken one in the throat. Two others wearing boilersuits and steel-toe boots had each been shot in the chest. On a sodden rug beside the stone hearth lay a biker in leathers with a spiderweb bullet hole punched through the mirrored visor of his full-face helmet and the helmet was flooded. Blood everywhere.

'No wallets, no licences,' Lynch said. 'No ID at all.'

Carlin looked at the suited man dead on the chesterfield, holding the Ruger pistol. He looked about the doorway he and Lynch were standing in and then behind them at the door across the hallway pelted with bullet holes. He looked at the floor in the hallway and the console table under which the camera and canisters had been found.

'Get these developed.' He handed Lynch the plastic bag.

They stepped out of the shooting box and into the gritty light of a vast northern moor. Cold wind. Dawn sun boiled low in the sky yet offered only cold light and long shadows. A helicopter hung nailed to the sky, blades stirring the air, and then it was leaning forward, nosing towards the horizon, and banking sharply.

'The air smells funny without the fumes,' Lynch said. 'Too clean. Never thought I'd miss the city.'

Carlin inhaled and looked around. 'I could get used to it.'

They milled about the moorland and then turned and headed back, slowly, absorbing the grim acreage about them. Exposed gritrock risen though the dried heather and crowberry shrubs resembled great scabs grown across the back of the land. Small dark birds like windblown leaves blew over the burnt-yellow moor grass. Deep drainage grip channels coursed through heath and blanket bog. On the horizon of that spectral garden rose distant scarps and the ruins of an abbey.

The shooting box was a grand double-fronted building of many rooms and a chamber. Stone tile roof. Four chimneys. Floodlight above the front door. Abandoned beside the building sat four vehicles: two Audis, a Ducati superbike with jacked-up suspension and off-road tyres, and a Scania flatbed truck laden with eighteen 55-gallon drums. A tyre stabbed flat on each vehicle had left them slumped in the raked gravel, the superbike fallen on its side.

At the gable end they stopped at the body of a suited man dead on his belly between an Audi and the shooting box.

'Looks like he got the furthest,' Lynch said.

'Apart from her and the baby.' Carlin pointed his thumb over his shoulder.

Lynch turned and looked across the moor to where the other crime scene, smaller yet no less grim, had been cordoned off. The mother and daughter hikers who'd found the bodies and made the call were talking to uniformed officers among a fleet of ambulances and cruisers, lights strobing vibrantly in the pale light.

The woman lay sprawled in a peat bog, pink hair flecked with blood flowing across the sedge. Ligature bruises clouded under the skin of her wrists and ankles. Scarfed about her throat hung a spit-soaked gag and a blindfold. A gutter dredged through her cheek as if by a chasing bullet. In her back, her latissimus, gaped a ragged black hole. This bullet had perforated her torso and entered what she'd been carrying. Mute in her track-marked arms lay a dead newborn. Both had been branded.

'Fucking men.' Lynch spat in the grass.

Carlin looked at him. 'Bury that shit now. You hear me?'

Lynch grunted and looked away.

'I mean it. Bury it now or it'll eat you alive.'

Clouds massed into mountains and their immense shadows crossed the moor and the temperature, already low, dropped another couple of degrees.

'One thing that doesn't make sense,' Carlin said.

'Just one?'

'There doesn't appear to be any money involved. I mean, if this is some trafficking deal gone wrong, where's the money?'

Lynch thought about this. 'Maybe the money side of the deal was made over the phone or online. The laptop.'

The helicopter came back and swooped in low, the grass careening in the blades' backwash, and then it was rising again and moving off, leaving behind a thrumming silence.

Lynch's phone sounded. He took it out and looked at the caller ID. Kat. He pocketed the phone without reading the text and cleared his throat.

'Just one of the lads.'

'I didn't ask.' Carlin was examining the dead man's outstretched hand. The wrist and digits bent in abnormal articulation. 'What do you think?'

Lynch put on nitrile gloves and sat on his heels in the blood-spattered gravel and inspected the splayed hand. 'Looks like his fingers were prised apart. Couple feel broke. Like someone was trying to take something from him.' He stood up. 'A gun?'

'Maybe.'

'So what we have here is potentially missing money and a missing gun.'

'Which means?'

'We're missing a man. Or men.'

'And maybe a couple of other vehicles.' Carlin nodded at the ground.

Lynch stepped back and looked at the marked-off tyre tracks intersecting gravel and grass. 'More off-roaders. Big. Probably a Land Rover. The others, not sure.'

The clouds shifted and the sun flared and hit the truck. They squinted at the gleaming steel drums loaded on its back. All empty.

'You think them people in the chamber were inside those?' Lynch said. 'Transported in them?'

Everywhere seemed to stop and fall quiet. A breeze in the downy cotton grass. The helicopter now a far-off murmur high over the distant abbey ruins.

Carlin didn't answer.

'Drums lined with Teflon,' Lynch said. 'I mean, what are we talking here, acid baths? They were going to dissolve them?'

Carlin palmed flat his thin grey hair and shut his eyes. He still didn't answer.

66

The Banskin brothers stood waist-deep in the river mouth under a pale dawn sky. Dark hair and beards dripping wet. The smaller of the two stood very still, bloodstained hands at his sides in the cold water, eyes shut. The larger one hulked nearby laving handfuls of brine over his head, light catching in the droplets and in the stones of the pilfered rings he wore on every finger.

Three blurred tattoos marked their left forearms. Old flogging scars criss-crossed their backs.

A dog barked and the men turned. On the crest of the riverbank stood a man about sixty with a Dobermann. With an expensive leather shoe, he distastefully toed their bundled clothes and canvas kitbags. He wore a wool overcoat and a flat cap and carried an engraved double rifle. A seigneurial air about him. The dog had a docked tail and cropped ears permanently erect and when it barked again, the man stroked its sleek head.

'When you lads are decent I'd like to talk,' he called.

While the brothers dressed in filthy clothes, the man, who went by Cyrus 'Cy' Green, shouldered his rifle and swatted midges as he looked out across the estuary to a remote hill range that had taken on the same watery blue haze as the brightening sky.

Then he spoke, telling of an 'unholy fuck-up' at a moorland shooting box the night before, and they listened and they watched, and when he finished talking, Dolan, the smaller of the brothers, pulled on a dark green oilskin poncho and put up the hood.

'Why you telling us?'

'Before any pigs could come snuffling through the truffle patch, I spoke to one of my lads. He was gut-shot but still kicking. Said someone was in there taking photos. A woman. Said he shot at her but doesn't know if he hit her or not.'

'So?'

'So I want you to find her.'

'Why?'

'I suspect she has something that belongs to me.'

Dolan knuckled a nostril and blew out a string of snot. 'What something?'

'What that something always is.'

The elder brother, Joseph, finally spoke: 'Animals piss on things to mark territory, to show submissiveness, to claim ownership.'

Cy squinted between the men. 'You're saying I should have… pissed on my money?'

They said nothing.

'I checked high and low and didn't find a penny. However'—Cy held up a driving licence—'this I did find. Was in a rucksack on the floor. Don't know if she's just stumbled into this shit or she's been playing us all along. Either way, find her, I believe I find my money.' He handed the licence to Dolan.

They looked at it.

Orla McCabe. Thirty-five years old.

'You know where she lives, talk to her yourself,' Dolan said.

'A message needs broadcasting loud and clear to any weaselly cunts who think they can cross me.' Cy took off his flat cap and touched his dyed-black hair and smiled with only his mouth, teeth small and grey, well used. 'Your eminent presence is that message.'

They conferred in silence while Cy looked west at the clouds gathering over the distant mudflats and the thunderous sea beyond. The dog hadn't moved an inch or taken its eyes off the brothers. It stood rigid in its steaming gloss coat while vapour from its breath wreathed its head. Cy glanced at the men out the corner of his eye and then looked away again, back to the mud-flats, feigning interest in the littoral wastes of the rolled-back sea.

With Cy looking away, Joseph bent at the waist and reached into the tall grass. The dog's head followed him. Cy turned back, holding his cap, and was about to speak when Joseph rose and swung the curved blade of a sickle into his neck and pulled him to his knees in the glasswort. The speed of the attack shocked open Cy's mouth and eyes. Cap and rifle hit the ground. The dog leapt.

Dolan put a boot in its muzzle but it recovered quickly and went for him. This time he kicked it hard in the head and it yelped and backed off. Joseph jerked the blade free in a welter of blood and stropped the dripping steel on his thigh, while Dolan knocked aside Cy's flailing hands and strangled the rest of the life from him, arterial blood running through his fingers. The whites of Cy's eyes clouded red as capillaries ruptured.

They hauled the body down the bank to the inlet and cast him out into the silted depths. Insects blowing out of the reeds on cellophane wings. They stood watching blood ribbon and disperse through the turbid water while the dog paced the riverside, baying and whining as its master went under. Incurious gulls soared the soft blue void on invisible axes. They threw cap and rifle into the water and then ascended the bank and retrieved their kitbags and went to the dead man's grey Land Rover Defender.

The vehicle was fitted with roof lights and a bull bar and sat on a dirt road beside the cat's cradle of a felled pylon dissolving to rust. Keys still in the ignition. Joseph started the engine and Dolan tapped Orla McCabe's address into the GPS. The Defender accelerated and then braked and a rear door swung open. Dolan whistled and the dog sprang soaked from the reed bed and galloped up the bank. It stood staring at him through the open door, head cocked in strained contemplation. Then it shook itself dry, barked once and jumped in. The door shut and the Defender vanished.

65

Six hours ago Orla McCabe was standing at her kitchen table looking at the money in the case. The money lay stacked in a block the exact size to plug the hole beaten through the middle of her life. She wiped her arm across her sweaty face and looked at the case itself. A brutal thing, deep and bulky, like something a paramedic would lug. Bright orange shell made from some type of thermoplastic polymer. Unbreakable, watertight. Black foam lining imperfectly cut to accommodate the money block. She shut the case and went upstairs.

In the doorway of the box room at the back of the house, she stood watching her baby sleep. A flickering street light intermittently laddered the room through the vertical blinds. At the cot she kissed her fingertips and touched them to the baby's forehead. The baby flexed a chubby paw and made a noise in her throat.

Orla switched off the TV in her bedroom and watched Liam sleeping fully clothed on top of the covers. Was she in his dreams like he was in hers? She often wondered this but never asked. Afraid of the answer. She was covering him with the blanket when he asked her the time.

'It's late,' she said. 'Has she been okay?'

'Yeah, she's fine. I've been calling you. Where've you been?'

She walked around the bed and held him. He reached out and stroked her shoulder. She pressed her cheek against his beard.

'You okay?' he said.

She said nothing.

'Get in bed,' he said. 'I can feel the cold coming off you.'

'Come downstairs.'

'What for? What's wrong?'

'I need to show you something.'

After she'd shown him what she'd brought home with her from the moor, she packed a bag while he called his Uncle Fran. She'd never met the man and Liam himself hadn't seen him in years but they'd no one else to turn to. They lived small lives. The phone call was difficult for Liam and no doubt for Fran given the nature of the call and the hour.

She watched him standing there in T-shirt and boxers, holding his neck and looking down at the baby's clothes scattered across their bed. He saw her behind him in the full-length mirror. She put her arms around his waist and leaned her head on his shoulder. They shut their eyes and swayed on the spot. As if nothing was happening.

'We must be out of our minds.' He broke their embrace and turned to face her. 'We're doing okay.'

'How can you say that with a straight face? Are you forgetting how much debt we're in? We had our house repossessed, our first home. You've got a month left on the job you're on and then what, another six-month contract and you're out on your arse again?'

'I'll find something else.'

'What about me? You think I'm happy emptying bins and cleaning toilets? You said so yourself, you can't take being bounced from pillar to post any more. Well, neither can I. It's demeaning. Our lives are built on sand. That money is stability.'

'We can't do this.'

'You can't work on building sites, living hand-to-mouth all your life. You can't do it. I know I can't. Not for the next thirty-five years.' Her eyes sharpened. 'Scum take what they want. Maybe now and then, we should stop being so pathetically nice and take what we want. You know what the worst thing is about having no money? It isn't that you don't own things, it's that you don't own yourself.'

He looked at her with an expression of anxiety and confusion that left her stomach cold. Her eyes softened.

'Look, that money's a lifeline,' she said. 'Think what we can do with it. Debt gone, like that. We could put her in a good school. Private health care. I could start my own photography business. You could go to college or do whatever you want. We could buy a house again instead of pissing our money down the drain renting. We could start again, Liam, start properly.'

She took his cold hands and kissed them.

'Do you want to slave away for some boss for the rest of your life who drives a car worth more than people's houses?' she said. 'Do you want to spend every waking hour worried out of your mind about money? Having a fit every time a bill arrives or the van breaks down or she needs new clothes. Do you want her to grow up like us? Slaves with no opportunities. Grinding away in thankless jobs for rich pricks and then numbing ourselves to death in front of the telly. Is that what you want?'

She didn't give him time to answer because she knew he could be persuaded. He just needed a push.

'And then she goes to that shithole school on the corner and the manners and good ways we've taught her make her an easy target because we should have taught her to be scum like the rest just to fit in. It's easy being scum because they don't have any ambitions or expectations, but we do. It's just our bank account says otherwise. Our bank account says we're as useless and hopeless as the filth we live beside. Ambition is a disease and money the only cure. With that money, we're better people. With that money, she gets to live the life she deserves.'

'How do you put that kind of money into the bank without people noticing?'

'We buy everything in cash.'

'What, for ever? A house? School fees? Are you serious?'

'I don't know.' She shrugged. 'Yeah.'

'We'd have to deposit it in dribs and drabs. Open up a few bank accounts.'

She squeezed his hands and he squeezed back.

'We need to go,' she said.

She got her phone from the living room windowsill and was putting it in her jacket pocket when the nightmare image of men in a van tracing her calls stopped her dead. She looked around the room and focused on the couch. The image hit again and she switched off the phone and set it under the middle seat and looked out the window. Nothing. Just wind, darkness.

Under the dull ochre wash of the street lights, they loaded their bags and the case into the loadspace of his old Transit van, the case wrapped in a bedsheet and stowed in the furthest corner. She got in the front with the baby while he went back to the house to lock up. A train thundered by over the high brick wall at the end of the street, a wall daubed in graffiti and topped with flakes of bottle glass embedded in cement.

A new world was unfolding in her skull. A world of immunity and choice. The dead weight of frustration and anxiety and pessimism rising, dispersing. Money worries that had run on for years now seemed trivial, easily solvable, hardly worth considering. Their baby's future now looked a colourful and bright place with a surfeit of opportunity and choice. For the first time, she felt weightless. She tried not to think of the infernal machinations that must have gone into getting the money into the case, the intended transactions, the logistical planning, the underground

19

meetings, the earnest promises, the smiling lies. She needed to focus on now, on their lives. Lives augmented.

The lights went out in the house windows and he emerged and locked the front door. He got in the driver seat and sat looking back at the house while absently putting on his seat belt. She helped him buckle up and then she locked the doors and he started the engine. She looked down at the baby awake beside her, tired eyes lost in the middle distance.

'I can't believe we're doing this,' he said.

She held his hand on the gearstick. 'It's for her, Liam, not for us. It's all for her. Remember that. It's all for her.'

The baby opened her eyes and saw them there and her face crumpled and she looked as if she were about to cry, but sleep swallowed her consciousness and she slipped back under.

Liam switched on the headlights and pulled away into predawn darkness. While he drove, Orla reached down into the passenger door compartment and carefully rearranged something in there and then sat back and looked out the window into the onrushing dawn.

64

Almost noon. The blinds in the police station were open but the city skyline was blocked by the courtyard walls that held the carriers and the vans and the cruisers below. The urban roar beyond resonated through the glass. Car alarms, blowing horns, roadwork, the airport flight path. After thirty-five years

Carlin was used to it. He wouldn't miss it when he was gone but he was used to it.

He sat alone in the office, drinking vending-machine chicken soup from a plastic cup, bifocals hanging on the end of his nose. He was studying a series of monochrome photos developed from the film canisters found with the Nikon camera in the shooting box. Photos of moorland and reservoirs, outcrops and gritstone walls, limpid brooks, moorbirds. Photos of an abbey in ruins. Photos of the shooting box's exterior. Photos of the vandalized and abandoned vehicles and their plates. None of the dead in the living room or the concrete chamber. Why?

He thought about this, picturing the suited man on the chesterfield aiming the gun at the doorway, the bullet holes, the positioning of the camera and canisters on the hallway floor. He guessed a dying man lying there firing a gun would probably prevent him from taking photos too. He picked up a pile of monochrome photos developed from another of the canisters.

Candid images of a woman, mid-thirties, sitting on a swing. Then a man laughing while driving a van. Another of her sitting with the man and a newborn on a blanket in tall grass, the photo taken at arm's length by the woman, the two of them smiling over the sleeping child, the low sun flaring behind almost darkening the woman from the image. To Carlin's eye something was wrong with their smiles.

He looked at the framed photo of his own family. Wife, daughter, granddaughter. They should not occupy the same abyssal plane as these photos. He knew better. He was putting his own photo in the desk drawer when Lynch came into the office, eating a bacon sandwich folded in a greasy napkin and carrying an envelope. He pushed the envelope across Carlin's desk and tapped it.

'There's the address,' he said.

Carlin opened the envelope and took out a sheet of paper and a monochrome photo of the same young woman, this time holding the baby and leaning back on an old Transit van. He looked at the van's plate in the photo and at the address scrawled on the paper.

'It's still registered to them?'

'Yep.'

'At this address?'

'Yep.'

'Mortgage?'

Lynch finished chewing and swallowing his sandwich before answering. 'Rental.'

'You tried calling them?'

'No answer.' Lynch wiped his hands and mouth on the napkin. 'Maybe they're out shopping.'

'What about the landlord?'

'A few late payments, nothing weird. Said she hasn't heard a peep from them in months.'

Carlin set down the photo and the paper. 'What about the camera in the chamber, the laptop, any luck?'

'Computer forensics is on it.' Lynch spun a couple of the photos around to face him. 'Black-and-white film, old school. They're pretty good. By the way, I looked into the phone records for the shooting box.'

'And?'

'There are none. It's never had a landline. They might have used wireless or something. We're looking into it. For now, it looks like if there was money, it was right there in the middle of bedlam. Speaking of which, I take it you heard about the passports.'

'What passports?'

'At the shooting box.'

22

Carlin took off his glasses. 'What are you talking about? We've just got back from the shooting box.'

'Forensics found them after we left. They didn't tell you? I thought they would have told you.'

'Jesus, lad, get to the point.'

'About fifty Eastern European passports were found taped to the biker under his leathers. Serbian, Latvian, Croatian. You name it.' Lynch looked at the photos and ran a hand over his expensive haircut. 'This is big, isn't it?'

Carlin picked up the photo again.

63

They drove with the baby asleep between them. The rumble of the engine and the road beneath them a meaningless drone, white noise. Orla sat looking out the passenger window at a vast petrochemical plant out on the edge of the sea. She felt drugged and unreal with lack of sleep and adrenaline. It was Liam who finally broke the silence.

'How do you go to take photos of a church and come home with a case of money?'

'It was an abbey.'

He looked between her and the road, his face stone. 'Don't, Orla. I mean it. We fled our house. Our home.'

'It's only a rental.'

'Only?' His voice rose sharply over the syllables.

'You've got to trust me.'

'You think I don't? I'm here, aren't I?'

'I know.'

'Then trust me.'

'I do trust you. It's just...I found it, okay? That's all you need to know.'

The road evolved boundlessly beneath them, neither source nor end.

'Whose is it? Orla, answer me, whose is it? Whose is the money?'

'Only bad people.'

'How do you know they're bad?'

'You don't want to know.'

'Did they see you?'

The baby woke and grunted and Orla hushed her, stroking her leg until she fell silent. Orla hated herself for creating another drudge to be exploited. But maybe she would do better than them, be better than them. Orla hoped so. But the apple seldom fell far. It was time to pick up the apple and throw it as far as she could. A sign for a services appeared and he pulled across the lanes and turned in.

She took the baby to the women's and changed her and then sat back in the van, listening to the news on the radio while he refuelled. Unable to stomach the constant sewer stream of fear-mongering and abjection from the airwaves, she switched it off and looked across at the payphone beside the entrance to the services. Three digits and it was over. Back to zero. No harm, no foul. Liam appeared and asked her if she wanted breakfast.

They sat in the food court eating sandwiches and drinking tea. He ate slowly, staring through the table, mind elsewhere. She ate quickly, watching customers, listening to their dislocated conversations. A babbling river of noise. The baby slept through it all.

Liam set down his cup and inhaled loudly through his nose and irritably ran his fingers through his hair and looked at her with an expression that said he was about to say something. He didn't.

On their way back to the van, she told him to go on ahead and she watched him walk off with the baby and then she stopped at a cash machine and withdrew all she could on their cards, maxing out each one. When she got back in the van, he was listening to a sad song from the sixties on the radio, something about cold lonely summers and saying goodbye. The sky clouded over and the temperature dropped and rain pattered the roof, the windows. A chill touched her and her skin cringed across her bones like a shying animal. He switched on the wipers and merged with the northbound traffic.

'Listen, I've been thinking,' she said, 'I don't think I should stay at Fran's.'

'What are you talking about?'

'If someone's looking for the money, I've got to draw them away from you. I don't know if anyone is, I'm just saying. In case. I'm not risking you two for any amount of money in the world. Don't look at me like that.'

'Where would you stay?'

'In here.'

'In the van?'

'Yeah.'

He looked at her deadpan. 'You're going to stay in the van?'

She shrugged. 'So what?'

'Yeah, that's not happening. If anyone's going to be staying in the van and drawing anyone away, it'll be me.'

She was about to protest when instead she took out the money she'd withdrawn and counted half and passed it to him.

'What's this for?'

'We spend our own money for now, not a penny of what's in the case, not until we're sure it's ours.'

'Why?'

'If it has to go back, which it won't, I don't want to owe anyone anything, not a penny. Okay?'

'Orla, I'm not—'

'Which exit did Fran say to come off at?'

62

The dead-end street of terraced houses was quiet and still but for a tabby vanishing behind a bin. It watched the Defender pull up and when the engine cut it leapt up a vandalized wall and slunk among shards of bottle glass. The Banskins stepped out hooded in dark green ponchos and accompanied by the Dobermann. Dolan tapped on the McCabes' front door. Joseph stepped back and studied the windows. Nothing. They turned and looked at the facing houses. A sweating postwoman on her toiling rounds. An invisible plane booming through clouds. Wheelie bins everywhere.

They circled the houses and went down a cobblestone alley. Joseph scaled the rear wall into a paved backyard and opened the gate, allowing Dolan and the dog entry. He shut the gate while Dolan tried the kitchen door. Locked. Joseph stepped back and then put his boot into the door below the handle, and Dolan seized the door to stop it swinging inward. They stood there in the ringing silence, listening, waiting. Then they entered.

They moved through the kitchen, looking in cupboards and on top of them, on the fridge, under the sink. Dolan poured the dog a bowl of water and tipped a packet of sliced ham from the fridge on to the kitchen floor. Joseph opened a door to a space under the stairs used for shoes and coats and an ironing board and he upended the lot and found nothing. He picked out one of Orla's T-shirts from a laundry basket beside the fridge and rubbed it into the dog's muzzle.

They moved into the living room and Joseph picked up two framed photos off the cheap coffee table in the middle of the room. One of Orla and a man smiling in a sunlit park, the other of Orla gowned and holding a newborn in the plastic light of a maternity ward. He took the photos from the frames and folded them into his pocket.

Dolan went upstairs. He switched on the light in a small makeshift darkroom. Pasting tables bordered two of the walls and in the heavy red light he looked at photos hanging pegged from wires over chemical baths, monochrome images of derelict hospitals and warehouses and sewers and churches. He left the darkroom without switching off the light and went into a baby's room. Stuffed animals of many species and colours. Cartoon beasts on the walls and curtains, the lampshade. He looked in and on top of the wardrobe, under the cot.

In the master bedroom he walked around the bed, looking down at the Defender through the blinds as he passed the window. He sat on the bed and looked around the room. Then he swung up his feet and lay back, filthy boots and clothes soiling the blanket. He stared up at a helical ceiling bulb, at the dust gathered in its shade, at the ceiling crack streaking from the light fitting to the wall and down behind his head. He breathed in the scent of perfume and shampoo and shut his eyes.

Joseph was in the living room studying a cordless landline phone's glowing screen when Dolan walked in. Joseph held out the phone and Dolan took it.

'That's the only number they called in the last twelve hours.'

Dolan pressed redial. The phone rang out. He hung up and looked about the room. Magazines and bills. A laptop. On a side table stood a lamp and a tattered black address book beside the phone's charger dock. He picked up the book and flicked through. Page after page of names and addresses and phone numbers, some scribbled out and rewritten multiple times as people moved, died, faded from memory. Several pages of pen-test scribbles and practice signatures. He looked again at the number on the phone and resumed scanning the address book. Under F he matched the number with Uncle Fran and there was his address. He factory-reset the phone and pocketed the book.

61

They got lost once but found Uncle Fran's place by mid-afternoon. A small house in wild disrepair surrounded by overgrown grounds. The narrow road outside, shadowed by great deciduous trees, lay unmarked and apparently much unused.

Liam parked on the empty driveway and took their bags across to the house and set them on the concrete step at the front door and gave a knock and then came back to the van. Orla walked around to him, carrying the baby. She held her close, rocking her, kissing her forehead, her nose, chin, cheeks. Fran came to the door. He was in his early sixties and wore his thick hair in a sharp side part with too much wax. Liam raised his hand. Fran nodded.

'I imagined him different,' Orla said.

'So did I.'

The sadness in his voice devastating.

'Listen, everything's going to be fine, okay?' she said. 'We lie low here for a couple of days, make sure if anyone's trying to find the money, they can't, then we're safe. You understand?'

'Yeah. Do you?'

'What do you mean? Of course I understand.'

'Good. Then we both understand.' He looked at the grass and frowned and then looked at her. 'I've been thinking. How would they know it was you who took it?'

'What?'

'How would they know it was you? Do they know your name? What you look like? Where you live?'

The gut-shot man on the chesterfield couch fires at her, and her camera and rucksack fall to the floorboards, film canisters fanning out in all directions. Another gunshot. Another.

'We're doing this in case they know those things, not because they do,' she said. 'We're just being careful.'

He looked beaten down, drained of life.

'We need to do this,' she said. 'For her. It's all for her. Remember that. Everything we do is for her.' She paused. 'I can't think of another way out of this hole. And I'm not backing down, Liam. Not for anything. Not for anyone. I'm sick of us being pushovers. That money in there, it's a gift. We've been given the grail.'

'No matter what I say?'

She shook her head.

He wiped sleep from her eye. 'That's that then.'

29

'Everything's going to be fine.' She smiled and held his and the baby's hand and kissed them both. 'I promise. Now go and introduce her to Fran. Just need to grab my bag and I'll be over.'

Liam went across the drive with the baby to Fran and Orla climbed up into the driving seat, started the engine and drove away without looking back. She couldn't. If she looked back, she'd have to go back. And that wasn't happening.

60

Carlin drove through heavy traffic to the address Lynch had matched with the Transit's plate in the photo. Wipers on. Radio playing low in the background. Lynch wiped a porthole in the window condensation and looked out. They passed a cobbled alley dim with rain and dull grey light and congested with wheelie bins, some fallen, some overflowing, some melted down. A hooded figure was carrying a child down the alley, which seemed to go nowhere.

'So, will you be gracing the Lodge with your presence this week?' Carlin said.

'Don't know yet.'

'You've missed the last two meetings.'

'I've been busy.'

'Oliver's been asking after you.'

Lynch looked at him. 'What do you mean?'

'He wants to know why you haven't been attending.'

'Why does he care?'

'Because he's Deputy Grand Master is why.'

Lynch turned away and looked out the window when he spoke. 'What do you think of him?'

'Of Oliver?'

'Yeah.'

'What do you mean?'

'I don't know. Just in general.'

Carlin sighed. 'Doesn't matter what I think. Kat married him. I've got to live with it.'

'But you're not happy about it?'

'She's not a wee girl any more.' Carlin swung the car left. 'Here we go.'

They parked in a cul-de-sac of compacted terraced houses. More wheelie bins standing before windows, some toppled, vomiting their guts across the ground. A train went by over the vandalized brick wall at the end of the street, its windows sick-yellow and choked with passengers.

Lynch shook his head. 'What a dump.'

They got out and tapped on the McCabes' front door. No answer. No movement inside. No van outside. Lynch knocked again and Carlin stepped back and looked up at the windows.

'What do you think?' Lynch said.

'Let's try the back.'

They took a slow walk around the house and along a cobbled alley, stepping over split bin bags and rain-mottled puddles that held the misery of the sky. The back gate opened without force and they glanced at each other. They crossed the paved backyard and inspected the kitchen door. A long, splintered indent below the handle and lock.

'Sledgehammer?' Lynch said.

'Or a good-sized boot.'

They put on nitrile gloves and Carlin found the kitchen light switch. They looked about at the mismatched furnishings. Lynch saw the bowl of water and an empty ham packet on the counter-top, a greasy stain on the linoleum.

'The McCabes got a dog?' he said.

In the living room he sifted through final-notice letters and looked at the empty photo frames on the coffee table, glass fronts and cardboard backs strewn on the carpet. He picked up the cordless phone. The wrong time displayed on the screen. He thumbed through the menus.

'Phone's been wiped.' He thought about this. 'We need to lift this for prints.'

Carlin went upstairs towards the red light that spilled across the landing from an open doorway. He paused and then continued on, slowly. He paused again outside the room, listening, and then stepped inside a crude darkroom. He put on his glasses and leaned into a pegged monochrome photo of urban ruin, an abandoned cinema, a gothic sewer system cut apart by shadows. He studied the photos, unable to work out their dimensions, depths. He scanned more pictures and then lingered on several shots of Liam and the baby. None of Orla.

In the baby's box room he stood looking at the music mobile hanging over the cot like a dreamcatcher. Shelves of plastic toys and stuffed animals. Colourful walls and curtains. His grand-daughter came to mind but he quickly cast her out. Not here. Too dark.

In the master bedroom he saw wardrobes standing open, full of clothes, and a bed stained with what looked like soil. He didn't hear Lynch come up behind him.

'I'm not sold on the idea of these people wilfully getting mixed up in this shit,' Lynch said. 'They've got a baby, for god's sake.'

'Maybe that's exactly why they got involved.' He regarded the bed. Like an optical illusion, the shape of a filthy resting body announced itself the longer he looked. He took off his glasses. He needed sleep. 'Desperate times call for desperate measures.'

'So what happened here? He goes out taking pictures on the moor, maybe hears gunfire and goes snooping round the shooting box, takes some pictures, gets shot at in the doorway, drops his camera…'

'Then what?'

'Then he comes home and is so afraid for himself and his family that they disappear. They get in the van and drive. Why doesn't he call the police? He's done nothing wrong. Got to be more to it than that.'

'Why wouldn't you report it?'

'If I was threatened.'

'There's that. What else?'

'If I've got something to gain by not reporting it.' Lynch tipped back his head and scratched his stubbled throat. 'Money.'

'Maybe that's where that gun went too.'

They went back downstairs to the kitchen.

'They're running because he knows he left something behind,' Lynch said. 'The film rolls. He knows we're on to him.'

'Maybe her.'

'What do you mean?'

'I think she's the photographer, not him.'

Lynch nodded slowly, thinking this over. 'Then she knows we're on to her.'

'And maybe not just us.'

Lynch looked at the busted kitchen door. 'You think those men who shot each other to shit were the head honchos?'

'Nope. And if these people have half a brain between them, they won't either.'

A wild-furred tabby appeared in the kitchen door and it froze when it saw the men and then it ran.

59

Orla sat parked in the van at the side of the road under dripping trees, roaring 'fuck' and screaming herself mute while punching the steering wheel. Then she drove on.

The spacious cab and elevated vantage point settled her somewhat and she drove in silence, no radio voices, no music, just the drone of the world revolving beneath her. Then she'd think of the case behind her in the loadspace and her rucksack on the moors, and her stomach would fall apart all over again. Terror wove narratives and erected visions before her, and she tried to look away but there was no looking away. Not any more. She'd spent too long looking away from the reality of her choking existence but this would not be the reality of her baby. Whatever it took, that baby's life would be better than hers in every way conceivable. Whatever it took. And right now, that meant looking.

Soon she arrived back on the moor. In every direction the charred and swollen wastes roiled away under the endless weathers of time to the skyline and beyond. Callous vegetation of rust reds and pale greens and hay yellows grew below cloud that scudded away across the bowl of the sky. A sky so hard it could rain stones. The wood-and-wire fence that randomly edged sections of road stood snagged with tufts of sheep fleece. She saw the silvery ghost of a hunting male hen harrier but no sheep.

She cruised through a wash of rain, eyes scanning that unplanted expanse for the crumbled abbey she'd photographed late last night before the lurching figure had led her to the shooting box. The eerie tracts of those desolate upland wolds somehow worse in daylight, harsher, more extreme, more hopeless. At least night had the civility to throw its dark blanket across the desolation and switch on the stars.

The abbey slid by out the window, staved in and roofless, now little more than an unremarkable relic in cold silhouette. She drove on, staring hard into the dim distance for the shooting box. A disc of light began descending from the misty fells and moortops, sweeping its way across the plains towards the road. She leaned over the wheel and looked up into the sky. A police helicopter pushing low through the rain took the swinging white funnel of its searchlight with it and the thunder of its engine gathered and rumbled in the hollows of the van.

Over a humped section of worn tarmac and as the road levelled, there was the shooting box. It soon became dreadfully apparent that this was as close as she was going to get. She'd hoped the place would be abandoned yet there it loomed, blaring with the strobing blues of police and ambulances and paramedics. Tripodal spotlights and crime tape and tents. Scores of uniformed figures posed in relative stasis by the movement of the van. The road leading to the shooting box had been cordoned off and traffic diverted.

She thought of her driving licence and camera in there, in the shooting box, strewn across the floorboards, and of the case in the back of the van. Her stomach cramped and her bowels dissolved, aching to be voided. The only thing that offered any comfort was if she were pulled over, the van had no links to the shooting box. And if the worst happened and she was questioned about her belongings discovered at a massacre? She'd say she left them at the abbey while taking photos, someone must have found them and taken them to the shooting box. She was just here looking for them.

She imagined pulling over and throwing the case into the moor. As a single woman she could risk the danger of keeping it, but with a husband and baby? Yet her family deserved freedom and choice and the chance to start again. Her baby deserved the world. She tightened her grip on the wheel and drove on, searching the hard skies for itinerant lights.

58

They were still a couple of hours from Uncle Fran's house and Dolan was sleeping, while Joseph drove and repeated with precise diction the recondite patois of the Shipping Forecast's broadcaster: '...becoming cyclonic. Good, occasionally poor. South-east Iceland. Cyclonic mainly northerly or north-westerly, becoming south-westerly...'

They drove country lanes, avoiding motorways and toll roads, stopping only for diesel and to let the dog out to do its business. The weather kept changing, one moment the sun flinching off the glass in brilliant streaks, the next heavy winds streaming in from across open flatlands, sweeping rain sideways through the air in dark waves and rocking the Defender. They passed through countryside and scrublands and mountains, dizzying valley drops, daisy-chained pylons striding the land, train tracks carving up hillsides and boring through living rock, mountain tributaries slaloming through scree, catching stray light and giving it back, and miles away, over a town crouched deep in a ring of hills, rain fell in strands like hair drawn through water. The storm continued directionless, lightning sourceless, and then exhausted itself and finally disbanded, and the sun briefly appeared only to bucket crimson light over colossal cloud-banks that stretched away to the rim of the world.

While Dolan dreamed bad dreams of Arden and Joseph mimicked the radio—'...four or five, occasionally six in south. Rough or very rough. Rain or showers. Moderate or...'—a phone rang and vibrated somewhere in the car. Dolan surfaced and opened his eyes and went through the glovebox and took out Cy Green's phone.

'Who is it?'

Dolan squinted at the glowing screen: 'A Henry.'

The phone finally stopped and Dolan chucked it back in the glovebox and shut his eyes but didn't sleep. Joseph resumed his mimicry: '...and Bailey. Moderate or rough. Rain or squally showers. Moderate or good. Occasionally poor in...'

57

In the evening Orla turned into a village and went to a quiet roadside pub and ordered chicken salad with chips and a strawberry-lime cider. She sat in the window with a view of the van across the way in a gravel plot under the swaying shadows of trees, a single amber street light struggling to light the car park. Beyond the trees the old sun was losing blood over the mountains, staining the slopes with gory run-off.

Who had found her belongings? Someone must have. They were right there in the shooting box's entrance for all to see. Impossible to miss. She thought of the red BMW and the silver Mercedes out cruising the moors in the dark. The footsteps she'd heard in the shooting box coming from behind an out-of-place steel door. The bloodbath. Gaped mouths and blood-drained flesh. The more she thought on it, the less convinced she was that police had found her belongings. Then who?

She ate slowly, listening to couples and families around her sharing stories of work and childhood, TV and politics, holidays and illnesses. She finished the cider while looking out the window at the van and wishing Liam and the baby were here. She'd never eaten out alone before. A waiter passed by carrying a tray of sundaes and she remembered the look on the baby's face when they'd first given her a taste of ice cream, the shock of the cold comically flashing open her mouth and eyes. Orla nibbled on a chip while the ghost of a smile drifted across her lips. The chill cider had run straight through her, and though she didn't want to abandon the van, she went to the toilet.

Heading back to her table, she held her face to a window to see the van. She could. And something else. A blue Ford Ranger pickup truck parked beside it. Its driver had almost anywhere in the entire place to park and had chosen there. She'd not seen the pickup at the shooting box last night. There had been four vehicles parked at the gable end and two cruising about the moors, and this pickup was not one of them. Then she saw the driver standing at the back of her van. He was a white guy built like a bear in jeans and black hoodie and was carrying a lump hammer and a crowbar. She just stood there, unable to think, unable to react, her mind unravelling, flowing out in all directions. Then she ran. She was running fast but it felt slow. Like running in dreams. Through the pub. Out into the cold night. Across the car park. Nothing but the sound of breathing and blood pumping through her brain. No idea what she'd do if she caught up to him. Her outrage powered her, filled her with a confidence alien to her. She reached the van but the pickup was already speeding away.

One of the van's rear doors hung open, locks wrenched apart. She looked inside. The case was gone. She uttered some absurd animalistic noise from the back of her throat and slammed the doors and leaned against the van with her head hung as if her neck were broken, muttering and swearing, sweat dribbling from her red hair. She walked back and forth, unable to think straight, her mind torn apart, a wind in there blowing the pieces around. People in the pub windows had stopped to stare. She kicked the wall of a back tyre and then got in.

Gripping the wheel, trembling, trying to think, trying to bury the hot shame and anger. She elbowed the door, raging at her impotence, repeatedly calling herself an idiot, until her head cleared and her heart rate steadied. That was it. It was over. Powerless to do a thing about it. Then she slid across the bench seat to the passenger door and looked down into the panel and saw it lying there in the dark. She picked it up and looked at it as if for the first time. The pistol she'd prised from the wooden fingers of a dead man.

56

Liam stood at the living-room window in Fran's home, staring out the dusty netting into the dark. Rain falling through the trees into the tall wild grass. Fran was sitting in an armchair facing the TV, feeding the baby on his lap mashed banana.

'So you're not going to tell me?'

'There's nothing to tell.'

'How much trouble you in?'

'I don't know.'

'Is it the police?'

'Probably.'

'Anyone else?'

Liam said nothing.

'And she's just left you both here, alone.'

'She hasn't just left me. She's…'

The baby raised her hand and squeezed the air for more banana. Need and want made flesh.

'She's what?'

'I don't know. Drawing them away.'

'Drawing who away?'

'Whoever.'

'Your mum and dad would have killed me if they'd known I hadn't been looking after you.'

'It's not your job to look after me.'

'That's not the point.'

'Well, they're gone now so who cares?'

'I should have been there.'

'I can take care of myself.'

'I should have been there.'

'You are now.'

Fran tried to smile. 'Do you remember coming here when you were a kid?'

'Not really. I mean, I remember something. I think I remember playing in the garden. Carol baking. Something like that.' Liam took out his phone and pressed the power button. Nothing happened. It was dead. 'Ah, fuck. Have you got a charger, Fran? I forgot to bring mine with me.'

'I haven't, mate. Sorry.'

Liam swore again and threw his phone on the couch and turned back to the window.

'You working?' Fran said.

'What?'

'I said are you working?'

'On and off. Why?'

'Doing what?'

'Brickie.'

'What about Orla?'

'She's a cleaner.'

Fran looked down at the baby. 'She's a great kid. Got a good appetite. Seems placid. What's Orla's family like?'

'We're it. She lived with her grandparents after her mum killed herself. She never knew her dad.'

'Where are they from?'

'Ireland. They came to Liverpool when she was little.'

Fran shook his head. 'I wish you'd tell me what's happened.'

'Why isn't she back, Fran? What the fuck?' Liam pounded the windowsill and then sat on the couch and immediately stood back up and took the baby from Fran and headed for the front door.

'Where are you going?'

'I need to get a phone charger.'

'Leave her with me. It's lashing down.'

Liam zipped up his coat around the baby and went out on foot into the cold night rain.

55

Orla sped north through the rain in the middle lane of the motorway. Hands frozen on the wheel. She focused on the red tail lights up ahead, trying to collapse the distance between herself and the Ranger. Occasionally the lights would vanish and she'd tense up and accelerate harder and then the road would curve and the lights would return and she'd breathe again. Mile on mile of wet road unspooling out of the dark. She'd been following an hour when the pickup turned off at an exit.

Down a country lane where the foundations of a new retail park were being laid. Earth cored and stuck with I-beams of structural steel and pipes and miles of wire. Black-yellow machines sitting abandoned in the mud. Fields and trees warping behind the glass. She passed the hefty carcass of a badger smeared across the ground. Verge reflector posts and sunken cat's eyes took and returned her light to guide her through that dark and perplexing journey.

Like her vision her mind had tunnelled. Peripheral thinking impaired. No extraneous thoughts. Nothing but the tail lights and the horror of having their lifeline snatched with humiliating ease. But she'd been humiliated before. This was nothing new. Debit

42

cards rejected. Credit card applications refused. Dinner tokens in school while the other kids used money. Getting out of a cab four miles from home with the baby and bags of shopping when she realized she didn't have enough. Cold water for months and ice forming on the insides of their windows because of a broken boiler. The mortification of the dole queue. Red-letter threats and then bailiffs and finally repossession. Snide comments from neighbours about how skinny her baby was, the implication shattering. She'd been humiliated before and she'd been pushed. She'd been pushed in school and she'd been pushed in work and she'd been pushed in life, but now with a gun and a purpose, she saw no reason not to push back. She was surprised by the sudden tempering of her spine.

A gypsy encampment came into view through the trees. She pulled the van over and killed the engine and the headlights and sat watching the pickup go among the camper vans and caravans, the vardos and donkeys, the shire horses, the dead bonfires. It pulled in beside a static caravan, its windows black and few. A moment later they came alive with a dim yellow glow and the door opened and a woman emerged wearing a black robe and holding a lit cigarette in her lips. The driver got out of the pickup, carrying the case by its moulded rubber handle. They spoke and then she turned and stepped back into the caravan and he followed.

The rain stopped. The temperature fell with the engine off. Orla's outlying thoughts and instincts came back into view, the most dominant being fear. But there was something else vying for her attention. Control. To take control of her life and slough this impotence. She took the gun from the door panel and looked at it, thinking things through with a sturdier, more encompassing mind. Practised holding the gun, getting used to

43

its sleek mass. But she had no intention of using it. She hoped the visual threat alone would be control enough. She felt stupid. Like a child playing make-believe. The gun didn't feel real. The situation didn't feel real.

The only thing that was real was the certainty that by doing nothing, she and her family would be nothing, there would be no translation from shadow to light, and the guilt she would carry would beat her to her knees and pulp her heart. She would crawl across the floor of the cave where the fire-thrown shadows were real and their casters always behind her. All that remained was this: the money in that case was the lifeline that would protect her baby from the suffocation of a life without oxygen. Nothing and nobody mattered, just the baby, and if this meant her and Liam being butchered on the altar of sacrifice to endow their baby girl with the life that they could not, so be it. So be it.

She got out and stood on the roadside and tucked the gun into the waistband of her jeans. The moon looked drowned in an eddy of bluish cloud. She looked out across the encampment. No movement save the mindless wandering of the horses and donkeys. She entered the trees and walked slow and hunched. She stopped among the trees to listen. Small life moving in the undergrowth had her jumpy and sweating, her eyes flitting through the dark. Moving on, heading for the encampment's edge. Wind soughed through the branches and leaves gently fell. Then the trees broke and the first wave of caravans hit.

54

Full dark when the Banskins found Uncle Fran's rundown home. Joseph parked a little away and cut the engine and the silence hummed. In the back the dog lay sleeping with its head pillowed on its paws, cropped ears upright like devil horns, tan eyebrows twitching. No vehicles passed on that quiet and unlit stretch of road. The GPS began to speak and Dolan switched it off. They watched the windows of the house. TV light playing blue-white against the netting. Dolan looked out the rear window, down the road they'd come from. Deep clouds over the horizon tinged orange with sodium vapour from the lights of a city that looked ablaze.

A man came out of the house. He was carrying a flashlight and walking slowly, almost shuffling in his backless leather slippers. He looked both ways down the road, sweeping the light about, as if looking for someone.

They got out and approached with the dog leashed on a short heavy chain found at the roadside earlier that day. The man took a step back when he saw the hooded figures moving towards him and shone the light in their faces. Joseph squinted and lowered his face, the rim of his hood veiling his eyes. Dolan raised his hand and peered through his fingers.

'Can I help you, lads?' Fran said.

'You're blinding us,' Joseph said.

The dog barked.

'We said you're blinding us.'

Fran lowered the flashlight, illuminating the ground between them.

'We're looking for someone.'

'I haven't seen anyone.'

'You haven't seen anyone.'

'That's what I said.'

'We heard what you said.'

Headlights appeared at the end of the road and the three men turned to look. The engine grew louder, the headlights brighter. The men and the dog stood still and silent watching the oncoming vehicle. The headlights swept across them, scattering the dark, and then the car passed, was gone, and the dark regrouped around them, over them. The men turned back to face each other.

'We're looking for someone.'

'Sorry I can't help.' Fran turned to walk away.

'You live alone?'

He turned back. 'What?'

'You heard.'

'Why do you want to know that?'

The dog lunged on its chain and barked at him. He took a step back and instinctively raised his hand, looking between the dog and the hooded men.

'Because we want to know if someone's going to hurt when they find Uncle Fran bitten and bled out in the grass there.' Dolan pointed at the grass.

Fran blinked. 'What?'

At Joseph's side hung his wood-handled sickle. Fran looked at the curved blade and then turned in his slippers to run back to the house. Dolan let go the chain.

53

Orla went stooped under the caravan windows as she crossed wet grass among hoof prints and muddy walkway planks. Some windows were lit but most were black portals to a dark yet deeper. Gas bottles strewn everywhere, some sucked into the mud. A swaybacked shire, standing beside an antique vardo covered in crude moons and stars, watched her and nickered and then lowered its great anvil head.

She squatted beside the Ranger and pressed her back to its double cab. The caravan spilled light from its windows under the pickup and across the mud she was crouched in. She unscrewed the dust caps of both driver-side tyres and let the air hiss out, the pickup slouching as it sighed. She stood between the caravan's door and its living-room window and looked inside. No one there, just a flashing TV sitting on an upended milk crate before a raggedy floral couch. She scanned the room but couldn't see the case. She ducked under the window and moved on to the next. This window was open an inch and the curtains were drawn but there was a swaying gap just wide enough to see through.

The driver and the woman in a cramped bedroom. She was sitting up in bed, smoking a cigarette over a saucer in her lap heaped with butts. The chaotic blinking from a muted TV at the end of the bed lighting the layered smoke that drifted about her. The driver was sitting topless on a plastic garden chair before a mirrored dressing table, the domed slab of his back facing the window, facing Orla. Open on the table before him was the case.

'We could take it and run.' He was looking at the money.

The woman looked at the back of his razored-bald scalp and then crushed her cigarette and set the ashy saucer on the bedside table. 'If you don't give Egan the money, he'll put you down and you know it.'

'It's not his fucking money. The deal collapsed.'

'He claimed it, Jem. He fucking claimed it.'

'I'm fucking claiming it.'

'Right, okay, tell me the plan. Go on. I'm dying to hear this one. Then I'm going to sleep, okay? It's too fucking late for this macho shite. I'm exhausted. I haven't slept in three fucking nights.'

Jem turned revealing a face that looked as if it had been chiselled apart and brazed back together by the blind. Strange tectonic clefts and seams. 'You want to hear it? Okay, okay. We walk out that door with this case, get in the pickup, and we fuck off and never look back.'

A pause before she said: 'You're fucking mad.'

'You got a better plan?'

'How about we stick to the plan that's been agreed?'

'And Egan keeps the fucking lot? Me and you get fuck all? Fuck that.'

'You owe Egan, Jem. You owe him. Least this way you get to keep your fucking ears. Or is that not good enough for you?'

'How about this: we take some. Yeah? We take some and we blame the fuckers who took it. Say they must've dipped their fingers in the pie. Lucky we found it when we did, eh? Cunts would have had the lot spent, wouldn't they, eh?'

Jem opened a drawer in the dressing table and took out a bag of cocaine and chopped out thick clumpy lines with a razor blade and snorted them back with barely a pause between.

'You know what, Jem, do what you like. You got six hours before

Egan comes knocking. Make a decision. The fucking right one. I'm going to sleep.'

She switched off the TV with a remote and lay back, pulling the covers over her and rolling on her side. He turned his back on her, on the window, and looked down at the money again, laid a large hairy hand flat on it. His humped upper body rose and fell with each breath. Then he shut the lid and secured the latches and left the bedroom and a shower came on.

Orla looked at the case on the dressing table. Looked at the woman, the window frame, the door leading to the living room. She looked at the case again and then went back to the front door and paused, studying the encampment before drawing the pistol from her waistband. She opened the door and stepped inside. TV playing low, shower blasting, a reek of tobacco and weed on the air. She carefully crossed the living room to the bedroom door and opened it.

The woman was breathing through her nose and making a clicking noise at the back of her throat. Eerily, though her eyes were shut, scleral crescents glinted. Orla leaned in, looking around the door, and saw something she couldn't see from the window. A newborn asleep on its back in a cot, arms and legs outflung like a pinned frog. The door to the shower hung open a crack, steam swelling out. She stepped into the room and moved past the baby and lifted the case off the dressing table by its handle. The baby had turned its head and was looking up at her. She looked at the woman and then at the baby again. The shower shut off. Abrupt silence strummed the air.

'Who the fuck are you?' the woman said.

Orla pointed the gun at her. She didn't know what to say. She'd never threatened anyone in her life. 'Make a sound and I'll...I'll shoot you. I'll kill you.'

Sensing the emptiness of the threat, the woman called out to Jem.

Orla ran.

Back through the living room, the woman calling out behind her, over and over, by now roaring Jem's name. Orla threw open the front door and leapt into the mud and took off. Past the steaming shire, startling it to its feathered feet where it nervously stepped about in the mud, swinging its gracefully elongated head. Lights came on in windows as she ran for the trees. Voices filled the night, loud and confused shouts. A cropping donkey raised its head to watch her pass with black eyes dull and gentle. Behind her an engine revved hard and then shut off. The pickup. Its horn blew a dismal rallying cry across the encampment. Then came the heavy slapping of soles in mud and on planks and a clarion chorus of voices.

She loped through the trees, gun in one hand, case in the other, its weight and gathering momentum pitching her off balance. Looking back, she half-expected to see a mob with forks and flames moving through the trees. What she saw was worse. Jem wielding a machete and entirely, terribly naked. Bare flesh flushed red and shiny. In the dark he looked like a skinned bear rearing on its hindlimbs. He weaved among the trees with tremendous athleticism for such indecent bulk.

She jumped into the van and tossed the case and the gun across the bench seat and pulled the door shut and went into her pocket for the keys. Out the side window Jem came careening out of the trees, vapour rising in threads from his hairless scalp and naked skin. She found the keys and started the engine and was accelerating as he swung the machete's broad blade against the window, glass resonating in its frame like a sheet of rubber. She sped off with Jem sprinting behind yet dwindling in the side mirror.

52

Dawn. The shipping container lay in the perpetual shade of a car factory at the edge of a dockside industrial estate. Smoking chimneys and the intricate pipework of chemical plants climbing the skyline. Parallel to the container sat a silver Mercedes saloon. A big black guy in a parka stood leaning against the container with his boot heel tapping the steel, phone held to his ear.

'Cancel the orders. It's over.'

'It won't be that easy,' his wife said.

'No, it won't, but we no longer have a buyer, so for now it's over.'

'The Serbs won't be happy, Egan.'

'I'm not happy.'

'What about Cy Green?'

'What about him?'

'He'll have people out looking for his money.'

'It's our money, not Cy Green's—our money. It's us lot who've had our heads on the block, not Cy Green, so fuck him. We dealt with the Serbs, we organized the passports, we organized the shipping. It's our fucking money. And we have people out looking.'

'You call what he did looking? I told you not to involve the pikeys. I told you.'

He lit a small cigar with a match.

'What happens now?' she said.

'Now? Now I get us our money.'

'How?'

He craned his neck and looked into the shipping container. 'He won't fuck up again.'

'You think?'

'I know.'

'You better be right. I'm warning you.'

He didn't say anything. Just smoked.

'We get the money, then what?' she said. 'We walk?'

'We walk.'

'There's no going back once I cancel the orders, Egan. We're burning our bridge to Belgrade.'

'Then we find another crossing.'

He flicked the half-smoked cigar and stepped into the container, dropped the phone on a desk beside two other phones, a scanner and printer, a set of two-way radios, a laptop, a high-end police scanner. Passports lay in stacks in a cardboard box. At the far end of the container, kneeling on the floor with his wrists lashed to his ankles from behind with plastic strap cuffs, was Jem.

'I'll get your money, Egan. You don't have to do this.'

'You had my money.'

Egan unzipped his jeans and walked back to the entrance and pissed a smoky stream into the hazy morning air, shook off, zipped up. His dull eyes were on Jem as he took a Stanley knife from the desk drawer. Jem strained, trying to pull his hands free, ropy veins surfacing in his worked-out arms and neck, and he tipped over.

'I'll get your money.' Jem spoke from the floor, looking at Egan with an expression lapsing between fear and rage. 'You don't have to do this. I'll get the bitch. I'll fucking kill her myself.'

Egan crouched beside him with his elbows on his knees. He looked down at him with a spider's cold insularity. 'I have to take something. Should have been money. You've tied my hands.'

Jem's wrists and ankles had begun to bleed with his straining, the plastic straps slicing through skin. 'Egan, listen to me, I'll get your money. I'll get it.'

'I know you will.'

Egan pressed his knee into Jem's face, pinning his scarred head to the damp plywood floor, and thumbed out a blade from the utility knife. Then he began. Jem barely made a noise during his slow disfigurement.

51

The figure crosses the ridge of the hill silhouetted against the stars. Lurching, knees buckling, veering out of control. It appears to be carrying something, cradling it under its arm as it staggers along. When it stops to look back, Orla quickly shuts off the engine and the headlights, afraid she's been seen. The figure lurches on and vanishes over the hill and stillness returns to the moor.

She's sitting in the van beside a wood-and-wire road fence, Nikon camera hanging from her neck since shooting the abbey ruins. Engine ticking. She was about to head home when that reeling figure out there among the blue folded hills stopped her dead. She looks out the windscreen. Sudden knife flash of a moonlit bird. Then nothing for a long time. Then headlights burning in the near distance and the sound of an engine. She instinctively slides down the seat as a red BMW with two men inside speeds by in the opposite direction to the figure. They don't look her way. In fact, they seem to be making a point of not looking. She sits up and watches the car's tail lights vanish within the heathery hills.

She gets out, fitting her rucksack over her shoulders and zipping her coat as she treks over craggy grassland and climbs the hill. On the ridge she stops and looks back at the van sitting there in the dirt, barely visible in the dark. She scans the moor. No sign of the figure. Just a point of light across a steep valley in the direction the figure came from. She waits. Watching and listening. Nothing but a hiss of wind. She descends the valley and fords the slimed steppingstones of a narrow stream. Soft green moss and the delicate trickle of purling water as it braids itself around half-submerged rocks polished smooth over millennia. On the other side of the stream she crosses a miry hag that sucks on her boots and then wades through an airy drift of cotton bolls driven on a peaty breeze. She moves towards the moortop light, the climb difficult in the cold and the dark, and a couple of times stops to listen. Wind. A solitary bird call. Nothing. She moves on.

A building rears as if from the earth itself. A stately shooting box. She sits on her heels among alien lichen cups and sips bottled water. A steeple of smoke rises from one of the four chimneys. The floodlight fixed above the front door casts an immense fan of white light across the raked gravel driveway. Off to the side of the building sits a small fleet of vehicles. She reduces the aperture on the camera to compensate for the intensity of the floodlight and takes some shots. Watches for fifteen minutes, locked in a vacuum of silence but for the occasional sound of invisible bird wings. She puts up her hood and breathes into her hands, drinks from the bottle again. When she approaches the driveway the water swings cold and heavy in her empty stomach. She keeps to the edge of the light as she moves forward.

A tyre has been stabbed flat on each vehicle. She looks through the tinted windows of two Audi saloons. No keys. A Ducati superbike fitted with off-road tyres lies toppled in the grass. No key in the ignition. She moves around a Scania flatbed truck laden with 55-gallon drums on its back. She looks around and then reaches and knocks on one of the drums. The steel rings hollow. She knocks on another. The same. Holding on to a side mirror, she puts a foot on the cab step and boosts herself up and looks inside. Dark, no key.

After taking shots of the vehicles' plates, she moves around the front of the shooting box, trying to see in through gaps in the curtains. The rooms stand lightless and still. With her back to the wall beside the open front door, she looks out across the floodlit driveway to the edge of the moor. The bell jar of the sky domes over her awash with stars. She inhales and steps inside.

Oak boards creak under her hiking boots. She stops in the burgundy hallway between two doors. One closed, the other standing open. She leans forward slowly and looks inside. A large, green-painted living room in which men lie dead among pistols and rifles and shell casings. Bullet holes and blood everywhere. The floor, the walls, the stone hearth, the globe bar, the bookcases. Even the ceiling. She steps back into the hallway and leans against the closed door and swallows. Thoughts storm. She steps back into the doorway and raises the camera and presses the shutter release. Nothing happens. Out of film.

On one knee she swings her rucksack across her chest and reaches inside and takes out an empty canister and removes the back of the camera and takes out the old film roll. She's inserting the new film when movement from the room flitters in the corner of her eye. A suited and blood-soaked man slumped on the chesterfield couch has lifted his arm and seems to be pointing at her. She looks dumbly at him, unsure what to think, what to do. She's about to say something, maybe ask him if he's okay, if he needs help, when a gunshot bellows through the shooting box and part of the door frame she's standing within erupts in a swarm of splinters.

She falls back into the hallway and crashes against the shut door, dropping the camera and rucksack to the floor. The camera slides from view under a console table and the canisters spill across floorboards

55

in every direction. She's scrabbling when the sound of footsteps down the hallway freezes her. Near the foot of a staircase that ascends into shadow stands another door. This one different, out of place. Not wood but steel. And someone is behind there. Another bullet slams into the door above her head raining painted woodchips down on her and she runs stooped back on to the driveway and throws herself on her belly behind one of the Audis.

Flattened against the gravel, she holds her breath. Heart pounding. Sweat chilling on her forehead and neck, trickling along her spine. Another shot rings out, followed by the deep, dull thump of a wall taking the impact. She lies there, waiting for the time between reports to increase. Minutes later, certain they've stopped, she's about to head back inside to recover her belongings when another gunshot peals. She presses her forehead to the cold gravel and shuts her eyes.

Sometime in her long waiting she looks under the slumped car and sees something she missed before. Around the other side, between Audi and shooting box, lies another man, suited and dead on his front in a groping theatrical pose like a man re-enacting his own death. Eyes clenched, mouth sagged, a pistol in his hand. A shot booms and she scurries around the Audi and levers the gun from his dead grip, bending and breaking a finger or two. She turns the gun about, feeling its shape, its weight. Surprisingly comfortable. Too comfortable. The flickering concern of fingerprints is threatening to absorb her when she sees something else.

A case sits squat in the gravel, deep and bulky and orange and freckled with blood. She unlatches the lid and opens it. Stacked inside are bundles of banknotes wrapped in currency bands. She quickly riffles through and estimates a monumental figure. Then she takes out a bundle and looks between it and the dead man and the gun. With a sunlike roar a plane shuttling souls by the hundreds crosses the roof of the night. Then silence and in the silence a shot sounds and she flees carrying both the gun and the case.

Back in the van she sits looking at the case that has replaced her rucksack on the passenger side of the bench seat. Her clothes steam. She slams her fist against the wheel. She has to go back to the shooting box. She has to put back the gun and the case and get her rucksack and camera. Maybe the shot man on the chesterfield is dead by now. But maybe he isn't. Maybe others have shown up or are on their way. The two men in the red BMW. Something dawns on her and she goes cold. She frantically pats herself down and then opens the glovebox, empties it out. She feels in the door panels and under the seats. 'Oh shit,' she says. Her driving licence is in her rucksack.

She cups her ears as if to keep her head from splitting open. Then she opens the door. She sets a boot on the footboard and sits there with her head lowered. She stays this way a long time. Thinking. She cannot risk it. Not yet. Anyone could be there or on their way. Someone already is there, behind the steel door. And maybe the blood-soaked man shooting from the chesterfield is still alive. She has no idea who or what these people are but she knows what they are capable of. The sight of a silver Mercedes speeding through the hills towards the shooting box takes the decision from her. She shuts the door and swings the van on to the road without switching on the headlights and accelerates into darkness.

50

Orla woke lost and confused. The van at once light and dark. Windows crammed with swaying branches that filtered a cherry-coloured dawn and cast formless shadows swinging across every surface. She was parked deep in a roadless wood and open in her lap was the case. She'd fallen asleep with her hand inside, touching the money, as Jem had last night in his caravan. Modern haruspices interpreting omens via wealth instead of entrails. She locked the case and laid it in the passenger footwell and climbed out.

The sound of birdsong and coursing water and creaking branches. She stepped around the scorched-black trunk of a lightning-felled tree on which colonies of bracket fungus grew, patiently decaying the heartwood inside with slow, soft rot. A floating seed head of midges scattered when she passed through them on her way to the water and regrouped behind her. She found a hidden waterfall spouting from a tangled mass of creepers and trees grown up the face of a high rocky wall, and the breeze off the falling water chilled her skin. Its plunge pool ran clear and in the stream-bed lay rust-coloured stones alive with the shadows of surface motion.

She drove out of the trees and along country lanes bordered with pink willowherb that demarked harrowed fields and fields of rape until she hit the motorway. At the first service station she came to, she went directly to the payphones and looked at Fran's home phone number scrawled on a Post-it. She took out some coins and held one in the slot. She needed to hear Liam's voice, to know he and the baby were safe, this crushing silence too much to bear. She let go of the coin and punched in the number.

It rang for almost two minutes before she hung up. She thought about this while watching people flow past and then she collected the coin and reinserted it and started dialling Liam's number but stopped on the last digit when the nightmare image from the previous morning hit, though now modified:

men in a van tracing his phone. She hung up and stayed in the payphone a long time, holding on to the receiver, head drooped, thinking.

'They're fine. Everyone's fine. They're following you, not them. They're safe.'

But she could not convince herself of this and she fed the coin into the dark and dialled again. Voicemail. She said she hoped they were okay and that she'd call again later. She made promises about everything being all right, about how they were doing the right thing, about how she would be back soon. Promise after promise. She didn't say where she was.

She drove on, doing all she could to dispel the images of Liam and the baby lying slaughtered on a bathroom floor. They were safe. Those running her to earth, they could not know where her family was. They could not. She cruised north with her arm out the window until the cold hurt. Slowing to assess a meadow of wildflowers bordered by desiccated trees and then speeding up when a nearby house or vehicle or farmer appeared. She bore on, searching, considering each parcel of land before moving on to the next. She'd know it when she saw it. Kestrels levitated beside the motorway, spying the acres before swooping in prodigious arcs. Then she saw the cemetery.

She turned off at the next exit and entered a small town and went to an outdoors shop and bought a sleeping bag and a battery-powered lantern and looked at a foldable camping shovel. Too small. She went back to the van and wrapped the case inside the sleeping bag and stuffed the sleeping bag in the passenger footwell, the loadspace no longer viable with a busted lock, and then went for something to eat in a cafe.

Sitting in the window beside a lethal-looking cactus on the sill, the van in sight, she ate a sandwich and drank a cup of coffee.

A young woman with a blonde buzz cut and a spike through her lower lip came to clear her table. Orla asked if she knew where the nearest DIY store was. The young woman said about two minutes' walk away and pointed her in the right direction. Orla drove there.

Save the old man sitting on a stool behind the counter reading the back of a newspaper, a huge unlit pipe held in his side teeth, she was the only person in there. Smell of sawdust and solder and creosote. He nodded at her and turned back to his newspaper. She asked for the shovels. He pointed and started to speak and then gave up and got off the stool, trundled around the counter and picked a shovel from a rack of half a dozen or so, moved back around the counter and laid the shovel on top of it.

'Fifty inches. Carbon steel blade. Light and strong. You want it?'

She picked it up, getting a feel for its weight, looked at the price tag hanging from the D-shaped handle and then set it down and took out her money.

The streets were bustling and she found herself seeing Jem lurking behind every passer-by. Her legs and groin had broken out in itchy hives and welts. That she'd been in possession of a life-changing amount of money for less than forty-eight hours and already been through so much left her depleted and terrified. She started the engine and sat there, looking dumbly at road signs under a sky choked with clouds that appeared unable to move. The signs meant nothing to her. She'd lost her bearings. She went back into the shop.

'I passed a cemetery on my way here. Somewhere near the motorway.'

The ironmonger looked up from his newspaper and took the pipe from his mouth.

'Do you know the way back to it?' she said.

He took a flat carpenter pencil and a sheet of paper from behind the counter.

49

Carlin sat alone at his desk with the Police National Computer open on his monitor but he was not using the database. He was going through a pile of unopened letters he'd brought with him from home. Credit-card junk mail, loan approvals, bills. Lots of bills. He leafed through them, occasionally opening one and then tearing it in four and dropping the pieces in the bin. Massive debts accrued over years he'd told no one about. Not even his wife. Specifically not his wife.

He took out his notebook and looked at a hand-drawn table of figures. He made amendments and additions. He calculated the figures, scratched out the total, wrote a new total six digits long. Six digits. The loan he'd taken out for his wife to go private for a radical hysterectomy sixteen years ago had spiralled out of control. She knew he owed money but he'd told her it was less than five grand to banks. Nothing to worry about. The truth he feared would leave him a widower. Money owed to banks, payday loan companies, and worse: the bulk owed to a loan shark with a sliding scale interest rate contingent on his pendular mood.

He laid out five credit cards on his desk and phoned the book- ies. His way out. He was halfway through placing a series of bets on the horses when he saw an envelope amid the mail with no address and no stamp, just his name handwritten across the back in red marker. He hung up mid-bet and opened the envelope. Inside, hi-res colour surveillance photos taken on a telephoto lens of him entering and leaving the station, getting in his car, talking to officers. His heart thrashed.

Leaning on his elbows and shielding his eyes, knees bouncing up and down under the desk, he called his loan-shark creditor. He said he couldn't get that kind of money by then. He said he needed more time. He listened, eyes squeezed shut. Finally he hung up. He sat there in a daze, his stomach cold. He picked up the receiver and began dialling another number and then slammed the receiver down into its cradle three times.

Lynch came in a few minutes later, carrying a coffee and a sheet of paper. He placed the paper on Carlin's desk.

'What's this?' Carlin said.

'An emergency phone call from Liam McCabe.'

Carlin reclined in his chair and read the transcript, out of breath with anxiety, an oven on his chest. He finished reading and shook his head. 'His uncle. Fuck. Where is he now?'

'At a local station near where it happened. They're keeping an eye on him.'

'Well, that's made our job a hell of a lot easier. How'd it happen?'

'He was bitten by a large dog, beaten, his throat slit.'

Carlin thought about this. 'Jesus. No mention of the wife?'

'Nope.'

Carlin read the transcript again, shaking his head as he folded the paper into his notebook. He looked out the window. The rainwater glazing the courtyard and the vehicles inside created a landscape of halogen white and for a bright and lucid moment, he pictured himself climbing out the window and falling. The ground flying up towards him. The impact putting out all the lights of the world. The image comforting.

'You okay?' Lynch said.

Carlin came to. 'What?'

'Are you okay? You look tired.'

'Didn't get much sleep.'

'Same here.'

Carlin put on his coat and took a deep breath. He looked at Lynch a moment too long and then looked out the window again.

48

Following the ironmonger's map, Orla drove down a single-track road lined with hedgerows along one side and a low drystone wall along the other. Beyond the wall sprawled the cemetery she'd passed. The cemetery lay on an incline following the rise of the road, a climb that ran up to dense dark trees in the upper field and the start of a forest. She drove half a mile until she came to a break in the wall where she stopped and got out of the van. Perfect quietude. Not a house or a vehicle or a soul in sight. She exhaled vapour in the cold air. Small birds darted in and out of the wicker of the hedgerow. She got back in the van and eased it through the gap in the wall into the cemetery.

She rode the sunken rails of the perimeter's rutted wheel tracks and then parked at the summit under a great lone oak. A view of the entire cemetery stretched out below until it reached a dark copse of trees through which ribboned the motorway. She got out. Somewhere behind the land to the west heaved the sea. East lay fields that shaded off into the dark humped shapes of the dales. Hedges and fieldstone walls ringed off the cemetery and carved the neighbouring meadows into cryptic grids. Myriad crooked crosses and canted gravestones, some graves newly excavated, some overgrown, some caved-in. Dead and fresh flowers bunched into aluminium pots.

Her eyes centred on a particular plot. The name on the gravestone was MILDRED HOBBS. She moved downhill and stood graveside. The decision formed quickly. She went to the van and took the shovel and the case and then moved back down to the grave and dug. The soil cold and crumbly, the digging easier than she'd imagined. She dug only a small hole, afraid of hitting the coffin lid after a horror vision of rousing Mildred Hobbs infested her thoughts. Lidless black eyes, witch-green skin, yawning mouth plugged with dirt.

Knee-deep in turned earth, she stopped and opened the case. That obscene trove. Yet each bundle of money offered another choice for her baby, another chance. She placed her hand on the hoard and shut her eyes. The life she could see for them right there, flowering iridescently in the dark. More real than this. More real than digging out a grave in some nameless hillside calvary. She closed the case and laid it in the world below and sat catching her breath in the cold grass. An electric hum from the motorway. She held a pile of cold earth in her hand, dark and damp, churned it through her fingers.

If she had to bury the case every day and unearth it every day, she would. If that was what it took to be a free woman, to have a free family, then that was what she'd do. And now, at least if they caught her, the money would be safe. She would plead ignorance and the money would be safe. Torture crossed her mind but she shook the terror loose. She couldn't deal with those thoughts, not here, not now. She leaned and looked at the case down there in the hole. Then she shovelled in the dirt and patted it down and scattered dead leaves over the soil to match the graves around it. Stepping back, she looked down at the desecrated grave and compared it to its neighbours. Indistinguishable.

She sat in the van under the shadow of the oak and tipped back her head and shut her eyes.

47

The Banskins went shop to shop in the town Orla McCabe had visited. Looming at the counters, hooded, dripping with rain, holding up her driving licence to let staff get a good look at their quarry. Some asked if they were police and wanted ID, and they would leave and start again in the next shop. None had seen her. Then one had. A young waitress in a cafe with a blonde buzz cut and a spiked lip. She said she'd served her breakfast.

'Then?'

'Then nothing. Wait. She asked where the nearest DIY store was.'

They entered the ironmonger's shop and stood at the counter, looking at an old man chewing on a calabash pipe and arranging cans of wood stain on a shelf. They didn't speak. They waited for him to notice them. Finally he did. He finished up and went behind the counter while adjusting his clean apron and looked at them.

'Can I help you, lads?'

Dolan held up the driving licence.

The ironmonger squinted at the photo and then looked at the men. 'So?'

'Where is she?'

'I didn't catch your names.'

Joseph turned back and locked the front door and flipped the sign to CLOSED. Then he went behind the counter and stood beside the ironmonger, blocking him in. Dolan drew a chisel-point knife and set it on the countertop. The ironmonger looked at the knife and slowly took the pipe from his mouth. Joseph looked down at Dolan, who stood on the customer-side of the counter looking at the ironmonger.

'She was in here.'

The ironmonger nodded, still looking down at the angular steel blade. 'She was. Bought a shovel.'

'To dig what?'

'She didn't say.'

'You see what she was driving?'

'A van. I think it was a Transit.'

'Where was she going?'

'I drew her a map.'

'Draw us a map, cartographer.'

46

Lynch sat alone in the cruiser outside the service station under a sky low and heavy, ready to spill its guts. He and Carlin were on their way to talk to Liam McCabe about the murder of his uncle. Carlin had gone in to get coffee and use the toilets, his old-man bladder on the blink. Lynch was on the phone to Kat.

'Does your dad ever talk about the cases we're on?' he said.

'He never talks about work.'

'Probably for the best.'

'He never talks about anything. I'm surprised he talks to you.'

'He hasn't got much choice about that, has he? Mind you, he does keep it strictly business. No small talk.' He watched her father through the service station windows leave the toilets and walk down a long corridor towards the cafeteria beside a neon grotto of fruit machines and arcades. 'He said Oliver's been asking after me.'

'What do you mean?'

'He wants to know why I haven't been to the last couple of meetings.'

'He doesn't suspect anything. Don't worry.'

'What did you tell your mum about your eye?'

'Said I slipped getting out the bath.'

'She believes you got a black eye getting out the bath?'

'I don't know. I think so. She hasn't said anything.'

'Let me arrest him.'

'Then what, he gets a slap on the wrist and makes our lives hell?'

'You tell them everything he's ever done.'

'We've been through this. I can't stand in his kingdom day after day, telling every sordid detail with no guarantee it'll even achieve anything.'

After a pause he said: 'You still haven't given me an answer.'

'I can't.'

'Can't what, give me an answer or leave him?'

'What am I supposed to do, just pack our bags and drive off into the sunset with you?'

'That's exactly what you do.'

'It's a nice dream but that's all it can be. He's a barrister and Deputy Grand Master, for god's sake. Do you honestly think he'd let us get away with humiliating him like that? We need to stop pretending this can work out any way other than his.'

'Fuck him.'

'Unfortunately for us, Oliver does all the fucking.'

He gripped the wheel. 'Don't talk like that. I can't stand the thought of…Let's just go, Kat. You, the baby, me. I get a transfer. We start again. I could give you everything. Let me give you everything.'

Carlin left the services, talking on his phone and holding two takeaway cups to his chest.

'Shit, your dad's coming. When will I see you again?'

'Soon.'

'Think about what I said.'

'I am.'

Carlin handed him a cup through the window and set his own on the roof.

'Say that again,' Carlin said to the phone. He took out his notebook and pen. 'How are you spelling that?' He wrote. 'Which means?' He wrote something else, finished the call, got in the car. 'Coroner said a woman and two men from the chamber at the shooting box had a kidney removed within the last month or so. Real botch jobs. They're surprised they lasted as long as they did. And they've found a tattoo on one of the men. Four letter Cs in the quadrants of a cross.' He read stiltedly from his notebook: '*Samo Sloga Srbina Spasava*. It's Serbian. It means: *Only Unity Saves the Serbs*.'

'Serbian?'

'That's what they said.'

'Might explain the passports.'

'Maybe. Let's go.'

Lynch pointed at the ceiling of the car and Carlin looked at him confused. Then he understood. He reached out the window and retrieved his cup from the roof. Lynch switched on the headlights and pulled out of the service station and on to the motorway.

'So, how's the family?'

'The family?' Carlin looked him over with mistrust. 'They're good.'

'Kat?'

'She's fine.'

'The baby?'

Carlin lit a cigarette and put down the window an inch and watched the young officer. He blew smoke out through the gap, most of which drifted back into the car. Lynch opened his window a crack.

It was not the first time he'd had the urge to tell Carlin he was seeing his daughter. The old man's inability to sense the trouble she was in was enraging. Lynch could feel himself about to say something, something that could not be unsaid. He took a moment and got himself under control.

'Since when do you smoke?'

'First I've had in fifteen years.' Carlin looked into the lit end and then finished the cigarette and flicked the butt into the rain.

45

As she eased the van out through the cemetery and back on to the single-track road, Orla looked across at the lonely grave of Mildred Hobbs, hoping the case submerged in the wet earth was as watertight as it appeared. She needed to get to a service station and call Liam. She was sick with images of him holding their baby aloft in offering to some mad-eyed and bloodthirsty god of old. She did all she could to slash the black paintings that hung from the walls of her mind but by the hour they grew more vivid and ghastly.

She was slowly turning the van when she glanced in the side mirror and saw it. Cruising slowly behind was a grey Land Rover Defender. When she came to a stop, it did too. It crouched raring in the lane, wipers and lights off, rain pouring over glass and paintwork. Then the passenger door opened and a man stepped out. He wore a dark poncho down to his knees with the hood up. The type worn by soldiers and outdoorsmen. The rim of the hood shrouded his face in shadow. He was followed by a lean Dobermann with erect ears. He picked up the chain looped about the dog's neck and took something from the Defender, what looked like a white rag, maybe a T-shirt, and he pressed it into the dog's face, letting it get a lungful of its scent, and then he sank to one knee and spoke to the dog. The dog started to bay and lunge at her van, pulling at the chain. The man rose, restraining the dog with a strong arm, and then he and the dog began moving towards her, the Defender rolling behind. Its full beams and roof lights bursting on almost obliterated them.

Like a small and frightened animal trying to appear larger, Orla opened her door and then leaned across the seat and opened the passenger door, hoping it would look as if two people were about to emerge. She twisted in her seat and looked out of the van. The diversion worked. The man on foot and the Defender had stopped and now the driver stepped out. He was dressed in similar garb but was altogether larger, massive. The man holding the leash looked back at the hooded behemoth and then at her van. He bent and removed the chain and released the dog.

She dropped the van into reverse, spun the wheel until it locked and floored the accelerator. The van's rear crashed into the hedgerow, jolting her neck, and as she found first gear, she spun the wheel the opposite way and accelerated, the sudden speed as she broke out of the turn slamming shut the passenger door. She was heading towards the Defender when the coursing dog stooped under the open driver door and leapt on the footboard and clamped its huge jaws on her outer thigh. The van swerved and she cried out as she punched the dog's head. Its legs scrabbling wildly on the footboard and her seat as it tried to gain a toehold. The driver got back in the Defender while the man on foot merely stood aside, watching as Orla fishtailed past. His face was thickly bearded and his leaden eyes burned deceptively bright with the van's headlights.

The dog snarled and jerked its head as it worried her thigh. Blood welled and wept through her jeans around the sunken teeth. The animal's forelimbs pawed her seat, its hindlimbs uselessly groping at the door frame. She gripped its hot skull and gouged her thumb into its eyeball, first dislodging the eye and then bursting it in a warm, runny yolk. The dog yelped and finally let go, dropping from sight. A damped bump as the rear tyre bounced over it. She leaned out of the van and grabbed the door handle and pulled it shut. A sharp turn appeared in the windscreen and she jumped on the brake. Her rear slid out and she spun the wheel and realigned and in the side mirror saw the Defender had turned and was accelerating towards her, headlights boiling through the rain as it gained on her. The lane straightened out and coming at her was the blue Ranger pickup truck with its headlights off.

'What the fuck?'

Between her and the pickup, the lane widened into a gravelled turnout. She pushed the van harder and at the last moment swung into the passing place and the pickup barrelled past, taking her passenger side mirror with it. She glimpsed Jem at the wheel, crazy-eyed and wearing something wrapped around his head, maybe a bandage. She'd entered the turnout with too much speed and was slewing back into the lane when she heard behind the deep concussion of the Ranger colliding head-on with the Defender.

44

Dolan stepped from the wreckage brushing glass from his shoulders and beard. The one-eyed dog limped about him, whining and sneezing, its short coat slick with blood and rain. Dolan turned and stooped back into the crumpled Defender where Joseph sat with a gash over his eye, the brow deeply incised, a red wire running down his cheek into the dark tangles of his beard. Dolan hooked his arm around him and helped him from the mangled and steaming cage. The fresh air cleared Joseph's head and he pushed himself out the rest of the way and leaned against the Defender, catching his breath and orienting himself. He stood straight and stretched his back, rolled his shoulders, cracked his neck.

Dolan was picking glass from Joseph's beard in a perverse act of simian grooming when a gunshot exploded the silence, followed by the damp sound of Dolan's forearm taking the impact. He held his arm aloft by the elbow and looked at the hole punched though his sleeve and the quickly spreading blood. Another shot tore off his nose in profile and he tottered back, holding his face, and hit the drystone wall. All in the same motion, Joseph crouched, drew a hawkbill knife and lurched around the Defender. He grabbed the bandaged head of the man pointing the Glock and cut his throat. He fell like rope. Joseph watched him on the ground, legs kicking and holding his own throat in both hands in an empty attempt to staunch the blood. He looked as if he were strangling himself. When he stilled Joseph squatted beside him and lifted the reddened bandage wrapped obliquely about his head. One of his ears was missing.

Dolan stood leaning against the wall in the rain, slicing the bottom hem of his poncho into bands to wrap around his arm. The grisly mess from his nose fanned down his front in a pyramid of dark blood and mucus. He breathed haltingly through his gaped mouth, struggling for air. His beard hung heavy and sopping like something pulled from a drain. He finished binding his arm and wiped his mouth and beard on his sleeve and then they got back in the wrecked Defender and Joseph tried the engine. The bonnet had concertinaed, only one headlight remained, the windscreen had cracked along the bottom, and the driver-side window lay in pieces on the seat and the floor. On the fourth turn the engine started. The one-eyed dog collapsed on its throat as it struggled to climb in on three legs. It lay whimpering in the rear footwell, its forelimb wrenched from its shoulder joint, the bones within useless and deranged.

They set out along the lane in the opposite direction from the hissing pickup and the droning motorway on to which Orla McCabe had fled. The chassis knocking. A length of pipe scraping along the ground. Dark fluid dripping from the undercarriage. Dolan clutched his damaged arm to his chest and tipped back his head, breathing through his mouth and swallowing lots of blood and mucus. He coughed and gagged and spat on the mat between his boots. Joseph, half-blind with blood, kept wiping his eye on his wrist while he drove.

43

Liam sat in a windowless room. Nothing in there but a scarred plywood desk and four plastic chairs. He was holding his baby daughter. His eyes red-rimmed. He looked sick and feeble. Before him on the desk stood an empty mug. The officer who'd led Lynch and Carlin to the room said he'd take the baby while they talked. Liam protested but finally let her go.

'Are you going to find who killed my uncle?'

'We're doing our best,' Carlin said.

'Of course we will,' Lynch said.

Carlin gave him a look.

The detectives sat on chairs across the desk from him.

Carlin leaned forward. 'How are you doing?'

Rain crashed against the station roof.

Liam said nothing.

'How's the baby?'

'We're fine.'

'Good.' Carlin looked at Lynch and then turned back to Liam. 'Listen, I'm going to come right out and say it. You know and we know why your uncle was killed.'

Liam took him apart with his eyes. 'I don't know anything.'

'I get it. You can't speak because you think if you do, you'll be putting you and your wife in it. But let me tell you something. You're already in it. Deep. I don't know if either of you realizes just how deep.'

'I'm not scared of you.'

Lynch set his elbows on the desk. 'We're not talking about us. We're talking about the people after you.'

'No one's after us.'

'We believe your uncle was killed by the people—'

'My uncle was killed by some lunatic who wanted to rob his house or something.'

'Nothing was stolen.'

'So?'

'So whoever did this had every opportunity to rob him and didn't,' Lynch said.

'Maybe they were distracted.'

'By what?'

'I don't know.' Liam picked up the mug and set it back down. 'By me. I found him.'

'Where's your wife, Liam?'

'Why?'

'When was the last time you saw her?'

'Couple of days ago.'

'And where is she now?'

'Are you going to find who did this?'

'We found a camera and film rolls at a crime scene. A trafficking deal, human trafficking. You heard about it?'

Liam frowned. 'No. Of course not.'

'It's been on the news.'

'I said I haven't heard about it.'

'Are you a photographer, Liam?'

'No.'

'I ask because when we had the photos developed, you and your family are in them. Is Orla a photographer?'

'No.'

'But she takes photos.'

'It's just a hobby. So what?'

'Old buildings, ruins. Things like that?'

He looked at them for a long time before answering. 'Yeah. Abandoned places.'

'Places like abbeys on the moors?'

'I don't know. Maybe. So what?'

'So how did your wife's camera end up at the scene of a crime?'

Liam rubbed the back of his neck.

'Why did you leave?' Carlin said.

'I never realized I was supposed to stay in the house where my uncle was murdered.'

'I mean, why did you leave your home?'

'I didn't leave my home. I went to visit my uncle.'

'The two of you close?'

'What's that got to do with anything?'

'We're just trying to get a clear picture here, that's all.'

'I hadn't seen him in a while. So what?'

'How long?'

'I don't know. A few years.'

'Five?'

He gave them nothing.

'Ten? Fifteen years?'

'So?'

'So the first time you visit your uncle in however many years, that same night he's murdered. And the night before that your wife's camera is found at a massacre. That doesn't strike you as odd?'

Liam watched his hands turn the mug on the desk.

'Were you with her on the moor? Do you know why you're being followed? Why you've become quarry for maniacs? Have you any idea about the madness you've invited into your home?'

'We always talked about leaving the city and starting again, living by the sea, putting the baby in a good school, doing all we'd dreamed.'

'There're snakes in the garden too,' Lynch said.

Carlin and Liam looked at him. He looked down at his notepad.

'I think they think you have something of theirs,' Carlin said. 'Something they'll stop at nothing to get. Tell us where your wife is and we'll put you all into protection, the three of you. You'll be safe.'

'Then what, we go to jail?'

'Jail? Why would you go to jail? You've done nothing wrong. You find something by mistake and you do the right thing and hand it in to the police. Nothing unlawful about that.'

Liam looked at the ceiling tiles, at the dry white lights. He shut his eyes.

'They've already been in your home,' Lynch said.

Liam opened his eyes. 'What? Who? How do you know?'

'We were there. They'd broken in.'

Liam looked like he might puke. 'Probably just kids. What were you doing in my home?'

'You need protection,' Lynch said. 'We can give you that but only if you help us. Only if you admit you need it. Where are you going to stay?'

Liam touched a scuff on the desk. Somewhere in the station someone was whistling, someone was shouting, someone was slamming heavy doors.

'Liam,' Lynch said. 'Where are you going to stay?'

'I'm going home.'

'We wouldn't advise that.'

'I'm going home. I've done nothing wrong. I've nothing to be afraid of.'

'Listen, you seem like nice people,' Carlin said. 'You love each other and have a great kid. If I was in your shoes, I'd have probably done the same and not wanted to talk to the police. No way I'd be giving back money that'd change my family's lives. Probably just some scumbag's money anyway, right? The temptation unbearable. Now all that'd be fine but for two inconveniences. One: you aren't being followed by only your shadows any more. And two: the money didn't come from some who-gives-a-shit drug deal or anything so pedestrian. It came from the sale of people. People bound and branded and transported like cattle. People forced into drug addiction and prostitution, sexual slavery, organ trading. Maybe worse.'

Liam dug his fingertips into his eyes and pushed them around.

His face livid and blotchy and suddenly gaunt. 'How is there worse?' he muttered.

Carlin glanced at Lynch before continuing: 'Based on the set-up where they were found, we believe they might have been imported for…violence.' He paused. 'I didn't want to have to say this but I think you're being wilfully ignorant of the fact that the money you're hoping to live the easy life with has come from the suffering of innocent people. You're not bad people, I understand, but money makes people do things they'd never normally consider. Fills them with stupidity and overconfidence. Changes their view of where they see themselves and where they want to be. I understand why you're scared of telling us anything. I get it. You feel you'll be betraying your wife and kissing goodbye to the good life. But you need to understand what we're saying. It's not us you need to be afraid of. What happened to your uncle, we're scared that's only a taster. This goes way up the food chain and the people at the top, they're not going to stop till their bellies are full. Is money more important than that wee girl having a mam and dad?'

'I already told the officers all I know about my uncle. And as for my wife, I don't know where she is and I don't know anything about any money. If I had money, I wouldn't be sitting here. I'd be on a plane heading for a beach somewhere hot.' Liam stood and pushed his chair under the desk and said quietly: 'Give me back my baby.'

The detectives watched him without response.

42

Orla limped trembling through a small town buried in the shadows of wooded hills. She hummed with an adrenalized anxiety. Blood had dried sticky down her leg and her heart pulsed grotesquely in the dog bite, a sickly hot beat. She went into a pharmacy and sat on a moulded plastic chair with her savaged leg woodenly extended, waiting for the pharmacist, who had her back turned, to notice her.

'We closed at six.' She turned and saw the state Orla was in. 'Are you okay?'

'I've been bitten.' She gestured to her sopping jeans.

'By what?'

'A dog. A Dobermann. I was hiking. It came out of nowhere.'

'You should go to the hospital. The nearest—'

'I can't. I don't have time. Please.'

The pharmacist looked at her watch and then for some reason out the window. 'Come behind the counter. I'll see what I can do.'

Orla hobbled behind the counter and sat on a wooden stool. The pharmacist picked boxes and bandages from the shelves and laid them out on the glass counter and then went into the back room for a glass of water and then again for a bowl of warm water.

'Lower your jeans.'

Orla did so with mild embarrassment and the pharmacist cleaned the wound with the warm water, gently squeezing the thigh to encourage the blood. The water in the bowl turned pink.

'You probably need a tetanus shot.'

The pharmacist dressed the wound and gave her painkillers. Orla took them with the glass of water and raised her jeans, using the counter for support as she stood to buckle her belt.

'You said a Dobermann did this.'

'Yeah, why?'

'I'd have assumed it'd be one of the lurchers out ferreting.'

Orla drained the water and set the glass on the counter. 'How much for all this?'

'Don't worry about it.'

Orla thanked her and was half out the door when she saw the first-aid kits for sale. She bought a box and more painkillers and a pack of antibacterial wipes. Favouring her wounded leg, she went limping through the rain back to the van. Street lights painting everything a gaudy orange, difficult to see through, somehow worse than the dark itself. She sat holding the wheel, thinking things over. Then she saw the pharmacist watching her through the window. Orla smiled and waved and started the engine. The pharmacist didn't wave back.

Orla rounded a corner and parked in an unlit alley. Rain rolling in filthy tides down the windscreen. She looked out the passenger window at the shattered remains of the side mirror and then got out and shambled about the town in the rain looking for a payphone. She stopped at an old brick bus stop with a slate roof and leaned on her thighs and breathed. Through a gap in the hills, among purling drifts of fog, the bordering forest thatched the foothills of a mountain whose summit stood under a sky that loomed low and Damoclesian. Off to the side of the mountain sloped the concrete spillway of a reservoir. She shut her eyes against the sky and felt the rain cold on her face.

Back in the dark of the van, she sat there behind the wheel cold and wet and exhausted, listening to the rain hitting the glass and the paintwork. She considered driving straight through the night to Fran's. Stopping for nothing or no one. Providing those after her hadn't found the grave, then the case wasn't going anywhere. She could go back for it anytime. But the thought of leading them to her family rose and a wave of anger shut her eyes and clenched her hands, dirty fingernails cutting crescents into her palms, and Liam and the baby were there, waiting for her in the deeps of her mind.

41

The Defender sat crumpled and steaming against a tree in the woods. Oil and antifreeze seeping through the damp spongy flooring of abscised bark and leaves and cones and needles. The Banskins wended slowly through the cold and clotted dark towards a light that shone dully through the dripping trees. Dolan held his arm in an improvised shirt-sling and breathed through his mouth, his ragged nasal hole curdling black at the edges. He kept retching swallowed blood. The deep cut in Joseph's forehead had left him blind in one eye and concussed. They pushed on through the unstable dark with the one-eyed dog hobbling behind, its broken foreleg swinging jointless like a sock full of stones.

They reached the light. The farmstead was a forsaken midden of decrepit buildings and the rusted carcasses of vehicles and ancient deadstock. Empty bottles of motor oil strewn about. Broken bricks everywhere. A reek of effluent from the saturated ground. They lumbered through the foul run-off and across the submerged course of planks to the dimly lit farmhouse. Dolan pounded on the corrugated-tin door.

Yelling and movement from inside and then the door was dragged open with a corroded scream. Standing there wearing a filthy green boilersuit was Tolmach, a man in his sixties with a leathered death mask of a face. He cradled in one arm an infant with neither jawbone nor ears hooked up to a clear bag on an IV stand. Its neck was thick and long and below the overbite where the chin should jut, the skin stretched pleated and confused with no mandible to grow over. A nasogastric tube taped to its cheek ran up a nostril below sloped eyes floating and sightless.

'Long time no see,' Tolmach said.

A woman called from somewhere deep in the house. He looked back over his shoulder and yelled at her to shut up and then shuffled outside and pulled the door shut, crushing the infant's tube.

'Nagging old cunt. I'd box her maw shut if it weren't for those milky paps of hers. I swear they're the only thing keeping us two kicking lately.' He grinned lopsidedly and jiggled the infant. 'Get over to the stable, lads. I'll be over when I'm over.' With faded eyes the colour of phlegm, he regarded anew the men and the dog. 'Shit. I wouldn't like to be in the poor fucker's boots responsible for this mess.'

They limped through the mud and the cold and across a field where a dead pear tree stood withered in the rain. At the rear brick wall inside the ramshackle stable, they lay on the concrete floor, their heads pillowed on their canvas kitbags. The dog buckled in a dark corner and weakly pawed the gelatinous mass of its burst eyeball clogging the orbit, oozed vitreous humour gelling the fur about the socket.

Rain slashed the entrance, obscuring the view of the farmhouse. The air thick with dust. There were two horses in the stable for six. One lay in a corner of its stall, shivering and sneezing plumes of misty snot. The other stood motionless, looking out at the rain through demented blue eyes ringed with too much white.

Tolmach appeared with a leather doctor's bag and unpacked veterinary equipment on to the powdery concrete floor.

'Listen, I'd let you lads sleep in the house proper like, but the old witch indoors, you know what she's like. She never quite got over what you lads did.' He laughed. 'No hard feelings, eh?'

Dolan's eyes were blank and unreadable. Like chips of dirty ice.

Tolmach set down the hydrogen peroxide and the syringe and took a bottle of whisky from the bag and handed it to him.

'Drink up, boyo. This shit's gonna sting.'

40

Lynch and Carlin walked around the crash site of the wasted blue Ford Ranger. Umbrellas and flashlights, coat collars turned up. Crime scene investigators went roaming among the tents and the steaming floodlights, while a forensic photographer documented the scene with a camera flash so powerful its light remained frozen on the air for seconds at a time. Ambulances and cruisers strobed their bleak blues. They'd got the call owing to the similarities to the murder of Liam McCabe's uncle. One prone corpse, its face planted in the ground, Glock clasped in its hand, wrists and ankles ringed with day-old ligature wounds, throat slit. While Carlin put on nitrile gloves and wrenched open the driver-side door, Lynch lifted the bandage around Jem's head with his pen and saw the great blood clot of a missing ear. Carlin shone his flashlight across the seat into the passenger footwell. Hammer, crowbar, chains, bolt cutters, ski mask, Motorola two-way radios. They walked the length of the lane, to the motorway and back to the crash site, Lynch trying to take notes, hunched over his notebook to block the rain, Carlin pausing every ten or fifteen feet to look around and study the land. Soaked gravestones bristled on the hill. They passed the wreckage and the body and followed the tyre tracks. Carlin traced the lane from the mindless humming of the motorway to his feet. Lynch looked back at the man on the ground under the forensic canopy, his throat a gory aperture. Carlin's eyes now on the oak in the cemetery that stood silhouetted against the night sky, now on the country lane hooking into the woods, now on a troop of toadstools that umbrellaed themselves against the rain, now on the rain itself as it pooled and seeped into the ground.

39

A uniformed officer drove Liam and the baby home. Holding the baby, Liam stood on his doorstep and waited for the cruiser to turn out of sight before opening the front door. A cold wind against his skin as if a window were open somewhere in the house. He stared into the dark, waiting for something, feeling something, something he could not articulate. A nameless dread. The baby woke and writhed as if in pain, arching her back and straining. He stood there on the threshold of their home with the door open, his back to the freezing night, hushing her. Her anxieties lulled. Finally he stepped inside and shut the door.

Silence and darkness. He moved slowly into the living room and closed the curtains and switched on the ceiling lights and the lamp. Empty photo frames on the coffee table. He swallowed. Then he went into the kitchen and saw a wooden chair from the small dining-table-for-two had been wedged under the handle of the busted back door. He picked out a steak knife from the cutlery drawer and with the baby clutched under his arm and the knife held out, he went room to room, searching, his heart giving out a rapid dry knock. In the last room he checked—their bedroom—he stopped dead in the doorway, staring at the dirt on the bed and the indented shape of a body. On Orla's side.

He went downstairs and sat on the couch, trying to settle them both, shushing her though she was making no noise. He coiled around her as if to absorb her inside him. After a while, no sign of danger, no sudden door slams or footsteps on the stairs or up in the loft, he plugged in his dead phone and switched it on. It sounded with missed calls. He listened to Orla's voice, her promises, and he wept. He called her phone. The call went to voicemail and he hung up. Realizing just how cold the house was, he switched on the heating and then fed the baby and made himself a sandwich and a cup of coffee. He threw out the dirtied blanket and pillowcases, changed the bedding and spent an hour or so getting the rest of the place in order. He knelt at the back door and looked at the busted lock to see how best to repair it. Then he remembered his toolbox was in the van, and he wedged the chair tighter under the handle and went and sat on the couch and watched TV. Not a moment penetrated, not a word. He didn't put the baby upstairs in her cot. He kept her right there beside him in her basket while he watched TV into the night. He left on the lights, the concept of darkness too much to take.

In the early hours the deep rumble of the train woke him from a sad dream of strange migrant birds flying directionless through fog, and he sat upright, trembling, staring at the closed kitchen door, the train already gone. He checked on the baby and then wrapped himself in a fleece throw from off the back of the couch and lay back down. The TV channel had ceased broadcasting and was now showing infomercials. He switched to *BBC News* just for the company but kept the volume low and then he sat up and listened to Orla's voice again. He called her phone again. Voicemail. He wondered how much she knew about the money, about the danger she'd put them in, and in her absence, animosity was filling the void she'd left behind. Yet his love and fear for her crashed against the growing bitterness and the sensation left him feeling he could puke. He should have told the police all he knew. He still could. Gripping the knife, he lay down on the couch and shut his eyes, and through the slow wheeling of the night, this thought pricked his mind and fingered his heart.

38

Tolmach came by the stable in the morning. Joseph was sleeping on his back on the concrete, mouth gaped at the rafters, dust in his hair and beard, eyebrow stitched and forehead bandaged, the concussion still seemingly reverberating through him. While blood pulsed painfully in the shredded stump of his nose and the crater in his forearm, both of which had been bandaged, Dolan stood in the corner, watching the staggers-stricken horse. The bullet had passed through the middle symbol of his blue-black forearm tattoos, which at one time he may have considered to be symbolic of something. Not now.

The horse reared silently and cycled its forelimbs as if in remembrance of the bloom of youth. Ill-shod hoofs landed on the concrete with heavy iron clangs and it trembled and collapsed in a lathery pile. Rain hammered the roof like falling rivets and guttered along its corrugations. And the cries of the infant cut through it all.

Tolmach eyed the dead horse and the dog, now lying in the stall with the staring horse, grim stablemates, though the staring horse had now shut its blue eyes and simply stood nodding senselessly.

'Not long now,' Tolmach said.

The shivering dog had refused food and vomited, hobbled to dark corners to vanish within. It was going the way of the horses.

'That car you left wrecked, can't leave it there,' Tolmach said. 'Gotta ditch it.'

They set off in his old van across the boggy ground and into the dark of the trees to fetch the Defender. Tolmach stepped into the rain wearing a clear hooded raincoat over his boilersuit and hooked up the Defender to his van with a short towrope. He ransacked the Defender's glovebox and found a flashlight, which he switched on and off before pocketing. He found a phone and brought it to the end of his nose, a murky eye turning inward as he focused on the screen. He bagged the phone and took a jack and a toolbox from the back and then got in his van, satisfied with his loot. He drove with caution through the hilly woods. Still, heading down dips the Defender would roll into the back of his van and Tolmach would grunt and swear with every shunt.

The rain stopped and the sun broke through the branches, heating up the woods. Steam rose from the ground and from the black wet bark of the trees and the air shimmered. Soon the woods cleared and they reached a vast and sheer sinkhole of near-perfect circularity around which trees stooped at the edge, dead roots stretching into air. Stagnant black water lay at the bottom of that great coring like a lens of obsidian.

They uncoupled the vehicles and pushed the Defender from behind to the rim of the basin. Dolan pushed with his shoulder and chest, his damaged arm held away. They paused on the drop and took a breather. Tolmach rested on the Defender, smoking a roll-up, inhaling deeply and holding his breath, locking the dark smoke in his lungs and then coughing and sputtering and laughing to himself. Dolan watched mute birds scratch the stony ground.

They pushed the Defender again and it upended, exposing its undercarriage before dropping out of sight. The dour hum of silence was shattered by the vehicle shattering the standing water. The water came alive in waves and lapped the black walls. In the murk of the waves' lowest troughs, Dolan saw the chassis of vehicles of many colours and ages, corroded in their drowning, veiled from space and time and memory. An amphoric wind blew across the chasm.

37

A truck rumbling by woke Orla. She sat up and looked around. She was still parked in the alley in the small town walled up in its chain of hills. Across the road a bird watched her and stropped its beak against the fence it was perched on and then flew off. For some reason a memory had followed her out of sleep and was superimposing itself across her vision.

Opening the front door one dark summer morning to a man when she was about ten years old. The man holding a box wrapped in shiny blue paper tied with foil bows. Lightning flickered silently over the rooftops behind him and he stood there staring at her for a long moment until her mother pulled her back into the house and shouted something at him and slammed the door. Maybe he was her father. She had no idea. Her mother had never spoken of him. Neither had her grandparents, who'd raised her after her mother had gone into the train tunnel one day while Orla was in school. For years Orla had considered it an act of cowardice. Lately she'd begun to appreciate the strength her mother had displayed, running headlong into the void.

After a short drive she came to a busy tree-lined street where she found a parking space outside a bakery crushed between an estate agent and a charity shop with romance novels and a chess set in the window. Exposed in the sharp morning light, the town appeared to be built mostly from limestone, shops and houses alike. She bought a takeaway coffee from the bakery and stood leaning against the van, her weight on her good leg. She swallowed some painkillers with the coffee and then limped across the road to a payphone and dialled Fran's number. It rang out.

She slammed the receiver down. Stay calm. She dialled Liam's phone. He answered after three rings.

'Liam, oh, god, I've tried calling. Why's no one picking up? Are you okay?'

'Where are you?'

'I'm in...' She looked around. 'I'm not sure. Are you okay? Is the baby okay?'

'I found your phone under the couch. You'd switched it off. You'd hidden it.'

'It wasn't like that. I thought they could, I don't know, trace it or something. Wait, where are you?'

'I'm back home.'

'What? Are you with the baby?'

'Yeah, she's here, she's fine.'

'Where's Fran?'

'He's dead.'

She couldn't speak.

'They killed him,' he said.

'Who killed him?'

'Who do you think?'

'Oh, god.' She ran a hand over her throat. 'I don't believe this.'

'I've spoken to the police, two detectives. They're worried about us. They said we're in danger.'

'What did you tell them?'

'I didn't tell them anything. But they told me something.'

'What?'

'They told me it was a human-trafficking deal. People bought and sold. Like cattle, they said. They said they're used for sex and violence. What have we done?'

Pulses were jumping in her eyeballs. Eardrums pounding. People around her moving underwater.

'I thought it was just, I don't know, drugs or something. Liam, I didn't know. How could I? I didn't know.'

'But now you do, can we live on money that came from that kind of thing? From all that suffering. Can we spend it knowing where it came from and still be happy?'

'It's different.'

'How?'

'Because we're good people. We'll do good things with the money. We'll raise a good family and give her everything she deserves.'

'People died for it, Orla. Fran died for it. Our daughter could have died for it.'

She leaned her forehead against the cold metal of the payphone.

'She keeps crying,' he said. 'I can't settle her. She misses you.'

Tears instantly formed. 'Don't tell me that. Please.'

'You promised you'd be back.'

'And I will be.'

'When?'

'Soon. I need to do something first.'

'Jesus Christ, what are you talking about?'

'I've hidden the money.'

'You've what?'

'It wasn't safe in the van. I hid it and…these people, they're everywhere. I need to make sure they're not following me, then I can get it and come home.'

'Fran's dead and you're carrying on like this is some fucking game. Can you hear yourself? Come home, Orla, now.'

She said nothing.

'They've been here,' he said. 'The people whose money you took, they've been in our home, in our bedroom, in the baby's room.'

'Oh, god. You've got to go.' Wiping tears across her sleeve. 'You can't stay there. What if they come back?'

'We tried that already.'

'Please, just go. One more day and I promise this will all be over. I promise.'

'I'm not leaving my home again, Orla.'

A police car cruised by. She turned away and watched its reflection slide across the windows of a Chinese restaurant.

'One more day,' she said. 'Just one more day, then I'll be...shit.'

Her credit had run out but she kept the receiver against her ear, eyes on the cruiser in the glass. It stopped at the traffic lights at a T-junction. The lights changed to green but still it didn't move. The lights changed to red and then back to green, and the cruiser still didn't move. She calmly cradled the receiver and, limping as little as possible, went back to the van.

She found a garage on the edge of town and filled the van with diesel and bought a newspaper and then drove winding country lanes, heading east in the general direction of the case. That unholy grail. Part of her was relieved to have seen the police. Maybe she'd wanted them to stop her, question her, find the money, wake her from this nightmare of her own making. Yet most of her was glad they hadn't. The lanes weaved through acre on acre of expansive countryside awash with rain. Clouds moving fast.

When an abandoned country house came along, she slowed and then pulled in and parked on a patch of weedy gravel. Windows smashed and planked. The grounds wild. Rusted scaffolding shored against one side of the structure. After taking a slow, painful walk around the premises to confirm she was the only trespasser, she squatted in the loadspace, swallowing more painkillers and looking out the doors back along the road she'd come from. Trees and bushes swaying. Leaves sucking across the black wet road. She could feel something coming, something along that road.

She shut the doors and switched on the lantern she'd hung overhead and leaned against the bulkhead, flipping through the newspaper until she found an article headlined: MOORLAND MASSACRE. All bodies remained unidentified. Several unspecified leads being followed. No mention of missing money. Crucially: no mention of her. She didn't know what to make of these stark omissions. She read to the end of the article and two words hit her hard: *human trafficking*. The police suspected human trafficking. Not anything like she'd imagined. Liam was right.

In a shallow part of her mind, an eight-bedroom mansion she'd cleaned appeared. Pool table, bars, cinema room, lap pool, Italian marble counters, landscaped grounds. At the time a dark envy had overwhelmed her, cowling her in resentment so bitter it shut off her senses and she stumbled numb through the days with a blankness of mind so complete she was all but dead. But now the memory of the mansion calmed her, focused her thoughts, validated her actions. She dropped Liam and the baby into that bright, clean open-plan living area and everything was perfect. She knew why she was doing this.

But that wasn't why she was doing this. She was not doing this because she coveted money and things, but because she was terrified of poverty for her family. In their late teens and early twenties, Liam and her being broke was okay because everyone else was too. It seemed the done thing, it seemed endearing, it seemed tolerable because everyone went through this phase: the young couple in love struggling to lay their own path in this cruel world. Things would start going their way soon, everyone hit on a little luck at some point. They just had to keep their noses bloody on the grindstone and one day they'd be joining the rest of the upwardly mobile.

Then their late twenties hit and nothing had changed except their first home—a smothering hole among the poorest in the city but still their first home—was repossessed. Being broke didn't look so endearing any more. People around them growing, moving away, having children, buying homes, saving money, getting promotions, travelling. Outlooks bright, prospects sunny. And now, in the middle of their fourth decade, it just looked embarrassing, lazy, wretched. They stood withered and frozen-footed in the standing waters of a grey waveless shore and watched a ship set sail with everyone they'd ever known aboard, voyaging towards a sunstruck horizon where serenity and opportunity lay.

Then she was pregnant. With an awing glow of empyrean light, the baby burnt away night from their day. The only light to warm their skin. Nothing mattered any more but her. What had loomed with great importance yesterday crumbled and blew away on amnesic winds, and all they'd once valued, or believed they should value, lay exposed as worthless. Now that they were working to raise a child, the menial grind didn't seem so humiliating and insignificant. Overnight they'd become hardworking, altruistic parents who led thankless lives for the benefit of a dependant.

But during those long, cold nights when Orla lay awake, acrimony broke back into their lives and began eating away at her again, tearing through her thoughts, continuing where it'd left off before the baby. She'd get out of bed and look at Liam, resentment like a clenched fist in her chest, resentment matched only by the self-loathing that had reawakened within her. Why wasn't he a go-getter? What the hell had she settled for? And why wasn't she? How can a relationship progress if both are apathetic? All relationships need at least one with drive, passion, grit. Especially when a child comes along.

She'd sit on the floor beside the baby's cot and shut her eyes and whisper how sorry she was for dragging her naked and screaming into this madhouse. She'd hold a warm little paw through the bars and whisper laments for creating something innocent that would one day know it was going to die. She hated herself for inflicting the agony of life on another who'd never asked to be here. Yet something came from this nightly purge of regret and sorrow on the cold floor of her baby's room. One night, breathless, needing air, she packed a rucksack and the Nikon F camera her grandparents had given her for her fifteenth birthday and she left for the moor.

She read the article again and swore and tossed the newspaper across the van and sat there on the rotten plywood floor, arms looped about her knees, head lolled, lit by a lantern that threw only a cold and brittle light. But when the dark was this deep, any light was better than no light. For her baby girl she'd thrown herself to the wolves. And how could martyrdom not hurt?

36

Egan sat alone at his desk in the shipping container, scalpel held between front teeth, scores of photos sliced from Belarusian and Slovakian and Estonian passports strewn about the desk. He was going through a folder of forged passport papers when one of his phones rang. It was Jem's wife. She was hysterical. He told her to relax and repeat what she'd just said. She said it again: Jem was dead.

'Dead how?'

'Dead how? She fucking killed him, didn't she? Cut his fucking throat.'

'Wait, who's "she"?'

'Fucking red-headed bitch that broke into my home and pinched the money. I want her blood, Egan. I want her fucking skull.'

'How do you know this?'

'Fucking pigs called, didn't they? What the fuck am I meant to do now, Egan? I've got a kid to—'

He hung up and opened a document and clicked Print. While he waited, he speed-dialled his wife.

'Why are you always right?' he said.

She groaned. 'What now?'

'Jem. He fucked up.'

'How bad?'

'Bad as it gets.'

'How do you know?'

'His wife just told me.'

'Fuck.' Something crashed in the background. 'Can this come back to us?'

A foghorn blared out on the dock.

'No,' he said.

'You sure?'

'I am.'

'How sure?'

'Ninety-nine per cent.'

'What's the one per cent?'

'Bad luck.'

'So what now?'

'You want something done, do it yourself.'

'You want me to come with?'

'No. You stay by the scanner and keep listening. Any mention of a Transit van, let me know. And from here on, use the two-ways.'

'Egan.'

'What?'

'Do not fuck this up. I'm warning you. You've backslid once. Do not let it happen again.'

He sealed everything in a safe bolted to the floor under the desk and put on a parka and took the printout and activated the container's electronic security system and moved towards his car. He was reading Orla McCabe's home address on the printout when he stopped and looked across the industrial estate at the Stygian grey-green mist flowing in from the sea. The floodlights of the chemical plant and the car factory hung suspended and haloed in the mist, and cast against the mist itself, in smoking effigies taller than the gantry cranes, strode the monstrous shadows of men.

35

Rainwater veining down the windows and a tawny light from the street lights washing into the living room. The baby lay sleeping in her basket next to Liam. He was sitting on the couch, the muted TV glowing in the corner, a weatherman towering over the country gesturing behind him at whorled thunderclouds crossing the land. Liam rose and paced the room just as the wind changed direction and rain hit the glass from another angle. He stood looking at himself in the fireplace mirror. Fran crossed his mind. Blue and cold and bled out in the grass. He gripped the mantel. Fran's face pummelled out of shape. Hands and arms chewed up by an animal. The glistening black vent gaping in his throat. He shook his head to dislodge the image, the scene, to raze it to the floor of his memory, and held his emptied gaze in the mirror until he could not.

Cold and needing coffee, he was filling the kettle at the kitchen sink when movement through the window in the backyard caught his eye. A black man in a parka striding towards the kitchen door and staring at him through the glass. Before Liam could react, Egan had put his boot into the kitchen door. The chair propped under the handle smashed against the fridge as the door swung inward. Liam dropped the kettle into the sink and ran for the living room, for the baby.

He was barely through the living room door when Egan snatched a fistful of hoodie and pulled, snapping back his head. His legs went from under him and he collapsed. Egan planted his knee in his sternum and grabbed his head in both hands and slammed it into the floor. The fight was immediately knocked out of him. His thrashing legs fell apart and his facial muscles went into a mudslide.

'Where is she? I know you know.'

Liam tried to speak but nothing came out.

'Where is she?'

'I don't know.'

Egan repeatedly punched him with both fists, one-two. He bled. Then he took Liam's hand and leaned over it, pressing down all his weight until there was a dull crack as the wrist broke and the palm lay flat against the inside of the forearm.

'Where is she? You don't answer me I'm taking an ear. You understand? I'm cutting off—'

The baby cried out from behind and Egan stopped and looked back over his shoulder. He rose and crossed the room and reached in the basket and lifted her out by a foot. He carried her dumb and dangling across the room and stood over Liam like some deviant accoucheur. He pressed his boot heel into Liam's neck, pinning him to the carpet.

'Look at me. Open your eyes. Look at me.'

Liam looked and saw the baby hanging inverted overhead, her face purpling. No longer semi-conscious, he reached up with his unbroken hand. He had become a simmering mass of energy. Egan pressed his boot harder into his neck and Liam gripped the ankle and bared his teeth.

'I can finish boiling that kettle. Do you understand what I'm telling you?'

'I don't know where she is. She called but I don't know. She didn't say. She left us. She fucking left us.'

Egan looked around and saw a phone on the arm of the couch. While continuing to press his boot into Liam's throat, he picked it up and thumbed through the call history and dialled the last incoming number. After sixteen rings the call was answered. An old woman. He said he had a missed call from this number and asked her what the number was. She said it was a payphone. He asked where the payphone was located. She told him. He looked down at Liam. Liam's strained face wet and rapidly swelling, broken hand turning grey-blue. Egan dropped the baby.

34

The Banskins sat around a fire in the clearing behind Tolmach's stable, watching red sparks rise through the smoke. The corrugated door screeched across the way and Tolmach bumbled drunken through the dark and windy field carrying a battered mahogany guitar and three bottles of dark brown whisky without labels. He passed a bottle to Joseph. Joseph twisted it open and drank. Tolmach held a bottle out to Dolan but his eyes were shut so Tolmach set the bottle before him in the grass and sat on an upturned bucket.

'He'd a been a good brawler.'

Tolmach nodded at the smaller of the two charred ribcages leaning against each other and smoking in the fire. The dog's eyeless skull lay nearby in the grass, rags of flesh and pelt still attached to pale bone. He strummed the low-tuned guitar once and leaned forward, laughing, his furrowed face scarlet in the firelight. He flaunted his hand, wriggling bloodied knuckles in the wavering flames.

'Just gave the hag fucking whipping of her life. She said she should have turned you in when Arden and the others darkened the door. I said ..' He backhanded the air and laughed, which avalanched into a catarrhal cough.

Dolan opened his eyes. 'What did you say?'

Tolmach stopped coughing. 'What? Arden came by.' He took a nervous swig of whisky. 'So what?'

'When?'

'Week or two back. Still wearing that stupid fucking preacher's hat.'

A river of wind came out of the dark and ran across the field and the fire rumbled and flared and sparks spilled over the ground.

'He's looking for us?'

'Course he is. You know he is.'

'What did you tell him?'

'The truth. Said we hadn't seen you.'

'Then?'

'Then we gave them milk and they left.'

'You gave them milk and they left?'

'No harm done, eh?'

Dolan didn't take his eyes off the old man for a long time. Tolmach rubbed the back of his sweaty neck and looked away. Joseph was leaning back on his elbows, swigging whisky and holding it in his mouth before swallowing. He looked at Dolan, who finally turned and looked into the flames, his eyes slant little dishes of fire. The infant screamed across the night while Tolmach ineptly tuned the guitar.

'We haven't named it,' he said. 'Been a year since she shat it out in the bath. Why name it now? Why name the cursed? It'll only torment it. A name should befit its owner. If you're nothing, you're nameless. More owners should be told this.' He spat at the fire and it hissed. 'It laughed when it came out. Believe it. Scared the shit out of me. It hasn't laughed since.' He strummed an off-key minor chord. 'Got a brawl on this weekend, just like the old days. Coon and a big old Highlands fucker. Stay and watch if you like.' He strummed higher up the neck. 'Some music?'

He played into the night, pausing only to fashion roll-ups and smoke. Dolan and Joseph drank and watched the flames while cometary slugs orbited the fire, silver tails streaking the grass behind them. Dolan lifted the bandage across his face. A breeze cooled the tainted air where his nose once was. Joseph played solitaire on his splayed poncho with a pack of fifty-one. The whisky ran dry and Tolmach set his guitar in the grass and wiped sweat from his forehead. He looked up at constellations he could not name and fell off his stool, out cold before he hit the ground. Wind gusted and the fire flamed up with a low whoosh and their shadows scattered into the dark. Later when the fire was nought but rosy embers, Joseph said he dreams of Arden.

'Same here. What happens?'

'He finds us. We're so afraid. He tells us to dash our feet against the stone.'

'Then what?'

'He takes us back there and buries us under the tree.'

'He won't find us.'

'He's throned in fire, you said so yourself. He leaves flaming hoof prints. His eyes burn in his skull. His forked tongue flicks and worlds end.'

Dolan picked up an ember and set it on the steel strings bridging the soundhole of Tolmach's guitar and they watched the strings incandesce and snap and the ember fall into the dark belly of the instrument and set it aglow from within.

'He won't find us.'

After releasing the blue-eyed horse and visiting the farmhouse for the second time, they left in Tolmach's van, bloodied from scalp to sole. The sound of Tolmach's howls at what he discovered in the room off the kitchen caught up to them through the van's open windows, but they ultimately faded, dissolving into the hazy air along with the night as the sun went up through the trees.

33

The snooker room was located deep at the back of the hillside manor. A brass telescope standing on legs of mahogany glared out of the wall-wide window across a pastel morning of hills and gorges and a blank pink sky. Sweet touched his slicked-back and prematurely silver-grey hair with his palm and turned from the window when his father spoke.

'Personally I couldn't give a fuck about Cy Green or the petty lucre—who steals my purse steals trash—but my sister's worried about him, so what can I say? She's been on the phone every hour since he went missing. And Henry's losing his tiny mind and threatening to kill every cunt under the sun. Apparently he's conducting his own search.' His father paused. 'I can't have this getting out. It'd ruin me.' He paused again. 'It wouldn't ruin me. It'd inconvenience me. It'd embarrass me.'

He laid his cue on the snooker table and walked around his blackwood desk to pour Scotch over the ice in his glass. Sweet noticed a tremor in his father's hand when he poured the single malt.

'It's eight,' Sweet said.

His father frowned. 'Eight what?'

'Of the clock. *Ante meridiem*.'

'What does one do with that kind of information?'

Sweet sipped black tea. 'How do you know this Orla McCabe has the money?'

'I don't. I'm only going by what Cy said when he called after the deal. If you want to call it that.' He unbuttoned his shirt cuffs and rolled up the sleeves. 'Cy found her driving licence right there in the shooting box and asked me to have a check run on her.'

'And?'

'Nothing. Boring prole nobody. I called Cy back to tell him the same, got no answer.'

The desk and wall behind it were strewn with framed photos of the old man at Big Pharma awards and gala dinners, shaking hands with people in boardrooms, behind podiums, before draped flags, with white-coated scientists outside a cuboid laboratory of black glass in Denmark, with two Chinese women before a vast building whose chrome signage read YUXIAN PHARMACEUTICAL HOLDINGS, amid a huge group of blank-faced suits at the Hotel Fairmont Le Montreux Palace in Switzerland.

'You think she was involved?' Sweet said.

'Probably not but it's too late for her now anyway.' His father was holding a framed photo and looking at it. He set it down and looked at Sweet. 'Cy said he'd have her put down regardless. But now, with Cy on walkabout and not answering his fucking phone, I have no idea if she's been put down or not.'

'Who's Uncle Cy using to find her?'

'No idea.'

'He didn't say?'

'He said whoever it is will be used to make a point.'

'Make a point. What does that mean?'

'It's Cy, it doesn't mean anything. He kept using the word *battue*, for fuck's sake.'

'Battue?' Sweet thought about this. 'Is he back on the coke?'

'Who said he was off the coke?'

Sweet took a leather notebook and mechanical pencil from his field jacket and wrote by the picture lights on the wood-panelled walls from which oiled portraits of his pedigree scowled.

'What about the police? They involved?'

'You don't read the papers?'

'How involved?'

'Peripherally. Nothing to be concerned about. Links they imagine can easily be…unimagined.' His father drank the Scotch and chewed the ice with massive capped teeth. 'Can you find them?'

'You know I can.'

'Will you find them?'

'Depends.'

'On what?'

'What am I supposed to do when I find the woman?'

'Get the money and put her down.'

'And Uncle Cy?'

'He's out of control, unpredictable. He needs to be taught to sit still.'

'This have anything to do with the livestreams I've been hearing about?'

His father's eyebrows came together. 'What?'

Sweet almost laughed. 'Yeah, right.'

His father licked his teeth. 'Maybe it does.'

'These videos, there's an international market?'

'The Mexican cartels wouldn't have supplied wealthy foreign nationals with an endless stock of maquiladora kids to take apart on camera for the past three decades if there wasn't. Europe's no different.'

'So it's substantial.'

'Like you wouldn't believe.'

'Oh, I believe it. So, Egan imports the meat, Uncle Cy makes the videos?'

'Something like that.'

'Imports how?'

'Egan and his bitch have intermodal freight transport links and dockers on their books who can alter container records.'

'Charons of the modern sea.'

'Easier moving people than drugs. The Colombians are using repurposed Russian submarines to move their filth these days. Submarines.'

'Okay. That tells me why so much money was involved. Are they traceable?'

'Which?'

'The meat and the streams.'

His father looked at the window. 'I don't know.'

'Do you think that's something you should find out yesterday?'

'I'm working on it. Anyway, I can no longer be associated with Cy, family or not. I used to be able to ignore his nonsense when he was just pimping, but this...this is intolerable. He's using family funds and that can't happen. No, this is the end. It's over.'

'Then say it.'

'I did say it.'

'Say it.'

His father looked at him. 'Put him down.'

Sweet flipped back several pages in his notebook and amended an entry. 'Can't imagine Henry's going to take this lying down.'

'Neither can I.' A pause from his father. 'Ah, fuck him. Henry's thick as pig shit, he'll get over it. Cy's easy to get over.'

Sweet finished his tea. 'Why's Uncle Cy dealing with a small-time supplier like Egan? You said he already had a supplier.'

'He does for pimping, not for this. And Egan's not so small-time any more. Word round the campfire, he even has a couple of nephrologists on his payroll these days for the kidney brokering. But this shit, this is big. This is where real money lives.'

The old man pulled the bead chain of a banker's lamp, flooding the desk with light, and took a key from his trouser pocket. He unlocked a drawer and took out a cardboard document wallet and then stopped, still looking down into the drawer. Sweet watched him, his father's mind elsewhere. Sweet tried to see what else was in the drawer but then it was closed.

'You still haven't said what happened on the moor,' Sweet said.

'We're investigating.'

'You do that.'

His father finished his Scotch and threw the glass against the wall. It came apart and rained down over a leather wingchair on which sat an old Polaroid camera. He stood very still with his eyes shut, face flushed, composing himself. Then he opened his eyes and tossed the document wallet across the table at Sweet.

'You've every resource to track them quickly. In there are all the details I could find on the woman. My contact got me a copy of her driving licence as well. Her photo's in there.'

'And what's this?'

'Some info on Cy. A username and password for the tracking software to find his car. It's been on the move since I last spoke to him, but now the signal's gone cold.'

'Wait. How have you been tracking Cy's car?'

'It's my car. I gave it to my sister last year, she gave it to him.' He picked up an ash and ebony cue and went around the snooker table. 'I had an OBD tracker installed in case it was pinched. Must have forgot to tell him.'

Sweet grinned. 'Why doesn't Henry know about this?'

'Why should he?'

'I don't know. Because he's his son.'

'So what?' His father spat on the carpet. 'By the way, if possible—and by "if possible", I mean don't ladder your tights trying—get the dog. Your aunt was intending to put it out to stud and you know what she's like.' He pulled a face and leaned over the table. 'Now watch this cannon.' He drew back the cue and potted a red.

'Lucky shot.'

'God himself once asked me to blow on his dice.'

Sweet leafed through the document wallet. 'Let's talk fees.'

32

Following the last GPS coordinates reckoned by the OBD software tracking Uncle Cy's car, Sweet found himself on a dead and isolated farmstead in the rain. He got out of his car, a Jaguar, and roamed among the rusted remains of vehicles and farm equipment. Snapped cables and nylon rope pressed vermiculate in the mud. A gagging reek of sewage. He stepped over a sunken cast-iron engine block and crossed a track of mucky planks as he followed the sound of hammering and sawing coming from the back of the farmhouse. He tried the handle of a corrugated-tin door. The door scraped open and he stepped into a fetid and flyblown structure stinking of poultry feed and rancid meat and something else. Something worse.

He drew a Beretta pistol and a handkerchief from his jacket and walked slowly through the rooms, handkerchief pressed to his mouth and nose to block the miasmic stench. The hammering and sawing getting louder. Foxed and peeling wallpaper hung from cloudy walls soft with rot. Dusty corner cobwebs. A filthy mattress leaning upright against a window blocking the light. Depending from a chain in the ceiling was a small birdcage with a live chicken jammed up inside. A glass tank on a sideboard containing a giant huntsman spider, a truly monstrous abomination, great spindly legs twisted at the joints and splayed forward, crablike. Stacked boxes of medical supplies and an IV stand beside an infant's fouled cot. He'd stopped before a closed door near the kitchen and was reaching for the handle when he realized the hammering and the sawing had ceased.

'The fuck you doing in my home?' A voice through gritted teeth. A voice so strained that spit foamed with its words.

Sweet looked up and pointed the gun at an old man in a rotten green boilersuit who'd emerged from the kitchen gripping a claw hammer. His eyes and nostrils were scaly with rheum, and his front was covered in blood and sawdust. It had congealed on his hands in dark clumps and between the folds of his weathered face.

'What's your name?'

'I said what the fuck are you doing in my home?'

'Looking for someone. Cy Green. Cyrus Green.'

'Get the fuck out.'

'He was driving a grey Land Rover.'

A sharpness in the old man's watery eyes, a slight turn of his head.

'You've seen him,' Sweet said.

'No. But I know who has.'

'Who?'

'The Banskin brothers.'

Sweet was briefly dumbstruck. 'As in Dolan and Joseph?'

'You know them?'

'Of them.'

'Well, that's who was here.'

'In that case it seems I'm looking for the Banskin brothers.'

'You and me both.' Tolmach wiped a leaky eye with the edge of his hand. 'Took off out of here with my van.'

'When?'

'This morning.'

Sweet lowered his hand from the shut door but kept the gun trained on Tolmach. 'Why were they here?'

'Wanted my help.'

'What kind of help?'

'They were fucked up.'

'What kind of fucked up?'

'You see a blue-eyed horse on your way up here?'

'I need specifics.'

'Dolan was shot. Joseph—'

'Wait.' Sweet took out his pencil and notebook. 'Go on.'

'Dolan was shot in his forearm and his nose. Took it clean off. Joseph was concussed. Had a gash over his eye.'

'What happened?'

'They'd been in some kind of crash.'

'A crash? You just said Dolan was shot.'

'He was.'

'By whom?'

'Fucked if I know.'

'How bad was his arm?'

'Superficial. Just missed his radius and ulna.'

'You a doctor?'

'I know animals. Besides the sin, we're no different.'

Tolmach spoke, Sweet wrote.

'This crash. Was it in a grey Land Rover?'

'Maybe.'

'If they're in your van, where's the Land Rover?'

Tolmach just looked at him.

'So, they need your help and you give it to them—why? How do you know them?'

'You a pig?'

'No.'

'You seen my horse?'

'No.'

'Who's Cy Green?'

'My uncle. And according to the wonders of the Global Positioning System, his car and phone's around here somewhere, with or without him.'

Tolmach slowly scratched his stubbly cheek. 'Wouldn't know anything about that.'

'But they would, right?'

'You gonna cut them down?'

Sweet didn't answer.

Tolmach stepped forward. 'I want them spiders bottled and brought to me. Whatever the cost. Already dug the holes.'

'What are you talking about?'

'Going to plant them cunts.' Tolmach took a long, thin knife from a pocket in his boilersuit and Sweet raised his gun. 'But not before I geld them first.'

'For a van?'

Tolmach leaned against the wall and looked at the floor. His shoulders rose and fell with his slushy breath. He looked back up. 'For what's in that room.'

Sweet turned his head to the shut door but his eyes stayed on Tolmach. 'What's in there?'

Tolmach just looked at the floor.

Sweet reached for the handle.

'Don't,' Tolmach said.

Sweet stopped and then reached again.

'Don't open it.' Tolmach coughed and sawdust billowed up, whirling in the grubby light. 'Don't.'

Sweet opened the door. 'Christ.'

He turned and walked out of the house. He stopped in the courtyard beside the rusted chassis of three stacked cars. The front door squealed and Tolmach emerged.

'You see why I want them spiders bottled? Before this day's done, I'll have buried four souls, swear to god.' He crossed himself. 'Two dark as death.'

Sweet slowly blew out a deep breath and then turned to look Tolmach in the eye. 'Would you like me to end your misery?'

'You what?'

'I have a deep and compassionate soul. You could almost say I was sent to you.'

'My angel of mercy.'

'If you like. Angel of mercy. I like that.'

'The only reason I have left to walk this earth is to hurt that two-headed jinn and you want to deprive me of that pleasure?'

'You may never sate your thirst for retribution, so I'm going to ask you one more time. Do you want me to end your misery? If you hear the bang, you're still alive. You won't hear the bang.'

Tolmach raised the gory hand gripping the knife. 'I got a red right hand.'

Sweet saw three hazy symbols tattooed on Tolmach's forearm. 'What are those?'

Tolmach pulled down his sleeve. 'None of your fucking business, that's what. See that?' He pointed across a muddy field where a skidsteer loader with a power-driven auger attachment at the front end sat beneath a lifeless pear tree.

Sweet looked at the shiny black-yellow vehicle at odds with the outmoded equipment lying about the yard. 'A rental?'

Tolmach concealed the knife but still gripped the claw hammer. 'Not that. What it's beside.'

Two mounds of dirt beside two bored holes. Big holes.

'Going to plant them deep,' Tolmach said.

'Those holes don't look long enough.'

'Long enough if you're planting them standing on their fucking heads.'

Sweet looked at the claw hammer and the boilersuit caked in sawdust and blood. 'Boxed or bareback?'

'Boxed.'

'That's what you're working on?'

Tolmach didn't answer.

'What wood are you using? Pine?'

'Aye.'

'A handsome softwood. I bet they're fine-looking boxes.'

'I don't like you.'

Sweet smiled. 'How do I benefit from your liking me?' He lifted his notebook and pencil. 'Right. I need two things from you. One: the make, model and number plate of your van. And two: the location of this crash they had.'

Tolmach told him.

Sweet was walking back to his car when he turned back. 'They didn't happen to have an ugly pinscher with them, did they?'

31

'Why would he have his ear cut off?' Lynch said.

Carlin just sat there, hunched over the gruesome forensic photos taken at the cemetery crime scene. They were in a booth in a quiet coffee shop frequented by police opposite the station.

'Maybe it was ritualistic, some kind of occult thing. Gang initiation maybe.' Lynch checked his phone and then put it back in his pocket. 'Or maybe just some pikey thing.'

Carlin was looking at photos of Jem, the big man with the slashed throat and missing ear. He was looking at the hammer and the crowbar and the chains and the bolt cutters, the ski mask, the Motorola two-ways. He was looking at the tyre-track photos.

'Three sets of tracks. Maybe this here'—pointing at the photo of the Ranger—'and another was chasing her.'

'Chasing Orla McCabe? You think she was there?'

'Those tracks match the van she's in, don't they?'

'They do. You think she's ditched them?'

A song started playing that Carlin remembered Kat and his wife dancing to at Kat's eighteenth birthday party. He wiped his eye and refocused on the pictures. 'I hope so. She's got a lot to lose.'

'Or more to gain.' Now Lynch was eyeing the flash-lit dead man under the forensic canopy. 'Is he our killer?'

'Could be. Or just some brainless lackey who pissed off the wrong people.'

Lynch considered the photos of the Defender's tracks. 'Same off-roaders as the moor. So, what are you thinking?'

Carlin glanced at his coffee and untouched salad.

'Well?' Lynch said.

But Carlin wasn't listening. He was looking across at the food counter. 'You know what I'm thinking?' He rose and picked up his plate. 'I'm thinking I deserve a fucking big cake.'

30

Sweet sat parked under a stone arch bridge three miles down the road from Tolmach's farm, dry-swallowing high dose methylphenidate and awaiting response from his contact, an old friend from RMAS. Water roaring beside him greenly foaming as it slid endlessly away. Low sun roosting in the trees. His phone vibrated with a text and three attachments. He read the text and then switched on the mobile printer on the passenger seat and wirelessly printed the attached police reports. There had been a crash involving a blue Ford Ranger. A mutilated male body found at the scene, throat cut, ear missing. The reports did not mention a grey Land Rover Defender. But he knew.

29

Gusting wind and rain had lashed and rocked the van all night. Orla lay curled on the sleeping bag, looking up at the cold and flimsy light of the swaying lantern like a woman sealed in an ark lost at sea. A frantic beat of rain on the roof. Mid-morning the wind and the rain stopped and the van fell silent. She sat up and lowered her jeans to her knees and lifted the bandage taped across her thigh. The skin around the dog bite had bruised brown-yellow, the wound jellied with curdled black blood. She swallowed painkillers with a bottle of water and cleaned the ring of punctures with antibacterial wipes and put on a fresh bandage and pulled up her jeans.

The words *human trafficking* were on her mind. The idea of turning herself in was on her mind. Would that fix or ruin everything? Would getting away with money that had come from the suffering of strangers be an easier pill to swallow than prison? Being wrenched apart from her family. The visits. The violence. The struggle for work afterward while ringing the leper's bell of a prison record. Seeing her little girl grow without the safeguard of money. What hurt worse than any imagined scenario was the guilt she held for the danger she'd put them in, and for Fran's death, and the anger and disappointment, maybe even hatred, Liam now undoubtedly held for her. She could take the self-loathing—she'd spent a lifetime honing it—but not the guilt, not him blaming her, resenting her. The thought of disappointing him broke her apart. And can a child respect one parent hated by the other?

She drank water and looked at her watch. Maybe she'd waited long enough. Time to get the money and go home. She hoped he'd left the house with the baby and stayed the night else-where. She hoped but knew he hadn't. He never went back on his word. She was lacing her boots when she saw it lying there on the van floor. A sheet of paper had been slid through the rear doors.

She picked it up. A blown-up photocopy of her driving licence. Handwritten across the top in red ink: LOST PET. She stood there for a long time, frowning in the dark, her stomach feeling as if it were flowing out through her bowels. She slowly opened a rear door. Outside in the grey light was a slim man in his thirties with slicked-back silver-grey hair and skin so smooth it looked as if he'd never shaved a day in his life. He stood leaning back on the bonnet of a Jaguar with his legs crossed at the ankles and his arms folded across his chest.

'Orla McCabe, I'm Millar Sweet.'

He raised his hand and pointed a black-yellow plastic handgun at her. Like a toy. He pulled the trigger and two barbed probes attached to conductive wires speared her stomach through her shirt and ran a violent current into her. She dropped to the floor of the van in galvanic spasms. Pain lashing out in all directions. A high-pitched squealing in her ears and then a welcome blackness pouring in behind her eyes.

She woke curled on her side on the floor of the van with her legs drawn up and her elbows between her knees. She tried to move but couldn't. Her wrists had been handcuffed across each other to the opposite ankle. Her stomach so compacted, so folded in on itself, she could hardly draw breath. Her limbs had numbed and she had the horrible sensation that she was floating foetal in the middle of the van.

'You awake, sleepyhead?'

She turned.

Sweet was sitting on the boxed-in rear-wheel arch holding the Taser, its wires still attached to her stomach. 'Good. You know why I'm here, right? Yeah, you know. Now listen up. Didn't take me long to find you and it won't take the Banskin brothers much longer either. They did it once, they'll do it again.'

'Who?'

'The Banskin brothers. They're after the money you thieved.'

'I'm living in a van. Do I look like I have money?'

He held up the newspaper she'd bought and pointed at the article. 'Now we're on the same page, tell me where the money is and I'll make sure it's only you who's killed. Your husband and daughter will be safe.'

She lifted her head. 'What did you say?'

'You're confused. I understand. Let me explain. What you've stumbled into is a land of perpetual dark. Flames don't take hold here and if they do it's to ravage not to brighten. You've thrown open a door on perdition and released—'

'I don't need your help.'

'My help? What? Oh, shit.' He covered a smile with the hand holding the Taser. 'You still believe you're in a place where someone can help you. Where people help one another. That's quite nice actually. Warm, innocent. It's comforting to know there are still people out there like you who think there's goodness in this world. You've comforted me. I feel even sorrier for you now.'

'I don't need your help or your sympathy.'

'Good. I'm here to offer neither nor could if I wanted. When those two rascals catch up to you, they won't stop at just you. They'll hurt your family. Do you understand? That's something I can guarantee. However, there is one thing I can do. You spill the beans and I can make sure it's only you who's buried and not your family. Here's how I see it.' He reached into his jacket and took out a bag of sweets, ate one, held out the bag. 'Jelly baby?'

'I'm trying to quit.'

'You possess humour. That's good. Many of the poor do. Helps them cope with their suffocating existence. If you don't laugh you'll cry, right? I get that. Anyway, here's how I see it. You have two options.

'Option one: you sit around with your thumb up your hole and wait for the Banskins to come. A word of warning: I have it on good authority that a man who made them chase, they tortured him and his wife for a week with someone on hand to offer medical assistance so the wretched souls couldn't even pass. You think about that.

'Option two: give me the money and under controlled and comfortable conditions, I'll put you down humanely. You must understand you're dead whether you give me the money or not. It's been foretold. Now it's just a matter of who you drag into the dark with you.'

He took from his jacket the pistol she'd taken from the dead man.

'Of course, you could do this yourself, sexy little PPK you have here, but a suicide attempt can be a messy and dangerous affair as you'll likely botch it the last second, especially now you don't actually have a gun.' He whistled as he pocketed it. 'But if I do the deed, I can then do your husband and daughter the service of informing those who are assessing the situation from above that the money has been reclaimed and that you are dust. The chase would be called off and your family would be safe.'

She lay still and expressionless, listening from a cold and numbing distance to the words of that strangely boyish psychopath.

'How does this work?' he said. 'As follows: I book us into a fancy-pants hotel. Say the Northern Sea. I order you a steak slab and a nice single malt and afterward, you crawl into the bath and take two bullets. One in the heart, one in the brain. If you hear the bangs, you're still alive. You won't hear the bangs.' He looked down and then back up into her eyes. 'Look on me as your angel of mercy.'

'You're out of your mind.'

'*Au contraire*, should you refuse my offer, favouring those two hellhounds catching up to you and your family, I believe it's you who's out of her mind. Now, I've searched this van high and low so I know it's not here, and so I'm going to ask politely: Where's the money? Do the right thing and take responsibility. Why kick against the pricks? For the sake of your family, lift this curse you've spat on them. Where's the money?'

She spat in his face.

He was tonguing the spit from his lips and swallowing it when his phone bleeped. He looked at the phone and then yanked the barbed probes from her stomach.

'My guess is it's somewhere near where they caught you, right?' He bent and picked up the filthy shovel off the floor. 'Somewhere in the cemetery? Am I getting warmer? Maybe I just look for a recently turned grave.'

He squinted at her but she gave him nothing. He took out a business card and a mechanical pencil from his jacket and wrote on the back of it and tucked it into her jeans pocket.

'My number and the address of the Northern Sea. The moment you realize you're not the master of your own fate and your family are the walking dead, you'll call that number and you'll give me the money and you'll thank me and you'll die.'

He reached up and turned off the lantern and then walked to the end of the van where he stood looking at his phone. 'I've several lines of enquiry to chase up, so for now I must love you and leave you. It'll give you time to brood.' He dropped out of the van and turned back. 'You seem sincere but I can't help myself. I really want to see you bleed out in a bath.'

From her torturous stress position, she listened to his freezing words and the more he spoke the more ice spread through the hollows of her bones and the chambers of her heart.

'You're already full of holes, light passing straight through. You just don't feel the absence of that light yet. You think you can survive out here in the cold and the dark but you can't. I'll make you feel the lack.' He ran his hands through his hair. 'Remember: He that is greedy of gain troubleth his own house.'

He slammed the door.

28

The silver Mercedes pulled up on a tree-lined street in a small town built almost wholly from limestone. Egan sat there with the engine running beside an empty payphone. He lit a small cigar with a match and got out. Knuckles swollen and bloodied. He stood beside his car smoking and looking about. A young man arguing over a parking ticket. Teens perched on a bench listening to music through a phone. Staff in a Chinese restaurant preparing tables for the incoming night trade. He went to the payphone and looked at the phone number printed above the keypad. He smoked and looked around. Light bluing. Silent birds fleeing sundown. The moon palely visible above the rooftops. He flicked the glowing stub into the air and drove on.

27

Men sat around the golf club's function room for their monthly Masonic Lodge meeting. Carlin was at the main table beside his son-in-law, barrister and Deputy Grand Master, Oliver. Oliver wore with pride his white gloves and chain collar and ornately embellished apron. The men were talking among themselves when the opening notes of Mozart's 'Lied zur Gesellenreise' began playing over the PA system to welcome the newest initiated member: the acned son of a private school headmaster.

After the pomp, Oliver leaned in to Carlin: 'No Lynch tonight?'

The mention of Lynch broke a dream Carlin had had during a febrile nap that evening on the sofa. He and Lynch buried alive in the cruiser in a landslide. Entombed in the airless heat under the interior light. Nothing but their hollow reflections in the black glass. Like being trapped in the head of a deaf-blind man.

'He must be busy. We've just started a big case. You know how it is.'

'Right. The business on the moors. I heard about that.' Oliver shook his head, muttering 'awful, awful' to himself.

A moment passed.

'Kat said you're buying a boat,' Carlin said.

'A yacht.' Oliver shrugged, indifferent. 'Well, a sailing yacht. A *small* sailing yacht.'

'Very nice.'

'I suppose.'

'Tell your face then.'

'I just…'

'What?'

'I don't know.' Oliver took off the white gloves and dropped them on the table. 'I feel like I'm losing her.'

'What are you talking about?'

'Kat. She's so distant. It doesn't matter what I do or say, she's just not interested. She doesn't pay me any attention, just keeps pulling away. I try but she just doesn't seem to care any more. She doesn't notice me. We hardly speak. Has she said anything to you?'

'You know what women are like.' Carlin supped his bitter. 'She's not going to talk to me about that kind of thing, is she?'

Oliver rose, finishing his drink, and patted Carlin's shoulder and headed to the bar, carrying his empty. Carlin drank his bitter and turned to the man behind him, staring into his pint.

'Brother Boyd, long time no see. How goes the Triumph?'

'Not good, Brother Carlin, not good at all.'

'No?'

'Can't afford it any more, mate. Thinking of getting rid.'

'Things must be bad.'

'Bit tricky bike-riding with one leg anyway.' He laughed bitterly and knocked on his prosthetic.

'What are you going to do every weekend?'

'Same as every other gimpy ex-soldier: drink heavily.'

'Fucking money, eh?' Carlin said.

'What else?'

'Same here.'

Boyd looked around before whispering: 'I thought being in the Craft meant they helped you out when you needed it.'

'A few quid here and there maybe. You should go right to the top and ask the grand old Duke of Kent for a loan. We've paid enough into the royal coffers, haven't we?'

'Not a terrible idea, Brother Carlin.'

They laughed without humour as Mozart's 'Maurerische Trauermusik' ominously faded in. They looked around the room at the tracing boards hanging from the walls, depicting the Square and Compasses, pentacles and skulls, fluted Doric columns, chequered floors and stars. The older Carlin got the more absurd this whole spectacle appeared.

'Christ,' Boyd said. 'Would it kill them to play some Hendrix? Just once, just once.'

'Maybe I could put in a word for you, get you in our place. Can't see them turning down an ex-serviceman.'

'You mean a desk job?'

'Not your thing?'

Boyd pulled a sour face.

'I'll keep a lookout anyway,' Carlin said.

'Nice one. Money, eh? The root of all evil, Brother Carlin, the root of all evil.'

They knocked their glasses together and listened to Mozart's final strains.

26

There was no music in the bar, just the noise of the crowd. Lynch sat in a window seat with Kat, his arm around her shoulders, his chin on her head. The skin around her eye was swollen and discoloured with bruising.

'You know they think I did this, don't you?'

'What?'

'The black eye. Everyone in here thinks I'm the prick who did this to you.'

'No one thinks anything.'

He glared at the drinkers regardless. After a deep gulp of Guinness, he said: 'He's a good actor. I'll give him that.'

She sighed and picked up her wine glass but didn't drink from it. 'What do you mean?'

'He's nice as pie at the meetings. The doting father and husband.'

'Of course he is. Do you think he'd risk exposing himself in there?' She brushed strands of black hair behind her ear. 'His whole life's an act.'

He set down his pint and turned in his seat to look at her. 'Look at your face.' He held her chin and gently turned her head. 'You're not going to tell your dad about him? About us? Hasn't this gone on long enough?'

'If I tell my dad he'll do something stupid and lose everything. I'm not having him going to prison for someone like Oliver. Can you imagine what they'd do to him in there, a copper? They'd take him apart.'

'I know, I know. I just…'

Seeing his fists clenching, his legs bouncing restlessly, she reached under the table and put her hand on his inner thigh, high up, and rubbed his groin, squeezing him hard through his jeans.

'My sexy toy boy,' she whispered.

He stared into her wet, red lips.

'Let's go,' she said.

They huddled under her umbrella and rushed through the rain to his car. Light from shopfronts and traffic flowing across the ground into the gutters. Horns blowing all over the gridlocked streets. A homeless man with a black eye and a broken nose lay slumped in the marbled doorway of a closed bank, plastic bags secured about his feet with elastic bands. Lynch squatted beside him and held his shoulder and said something to him and they shook hands. Before leaving, Lynch gave him a twenty and pointed him to the nearest shelter.

Lynch drove them to the edge of the city. All the way her hand tightly gripping him through his jeans. He parked in his reserved bay in the underground car park and they walked through numb fluorescent light to his minimally appointed bachelor apartment. Raw brick walls. Massive TV. MacBook. Xbox. Telecaster. The only photos: one of him with his mother and one of his police graduation. While he got the drinks, she leaned on the balcony railing and looked out at the yachts and cabin cruisers in the marina, its black surface lambent with flakes of light from apartment windows. The rain had stopped.

'Here,' he said.

She took the half-full wine glass and knocked it against his beer bottle. He joined her leaning on the rail and they nestled close in the chill and drank slowly. Music and laughter leaking from a nearby balcony. He finished his bottle and led her to his bedroom.

An hour later, after pleading with her to stay a little longer, he called her a cab and walked her down to the lobby, her heels loud on the tiles. The lobby was bright and silent and odourless. They sat on a leather couch between synthetic bamboos that stood potted in the corners. He spoke quietly in that echoey silence.

'I had to move in with my dad when my mum died. I hadn't seen him in years. He told me to be a man. Said if I was going to cry, cry in the car. He'd hand me the keys and I'd stay there all night, freezing cold and crying. I haven't cried since.'

She held his hand.

'I know I didn't cry when he died.'

He looked at her and then down at their clasped hands, and he sighed and shook his head as if embarrassed for saying so much. His knees had become restless again.

The cab arrived and she waved at the driver.

'When will I see you again?' Lynch said.

She took out the crucifix hanging from the chain around his neck and looked at it and then put it back.

'I'll do it.'

He was confused. 'Do what?'

'I'll leave him and be with you. I want to be with you. *We* want to be with you.'

'Are you serious?'

She smiled and they held each other.

'Stay the night,' he said.

'Let me get everything straight first. When he leaves for work, I'll call you, okay? I'll have mine and the baby's things packed and you can come get me.'

'You mean it?'

She nodded.

'I love you,' he said.

'I love you too.'

He drank another bottle on his balcony while watching a silent storm over the opposite apartments light the clouds indigo from within. His excitement at Kat's decision had become muted by the dream he'd had last night of the pink-haired woman and the child dead on the moor. Their skin covered in waxy grey adipocere. They were in agony and the woman begged for his help and the baby cried dark tears and could talk. *Help us.* He promised he would. He kept promising them.

128

Promise after promise. He'd woken in the early hours crying and disoriented, the TV on standby, the room dark, rain hitting the balcony.

He sat on the couch with his bottle in a tipsy daze thinking of the dead on the moor and the night he'd met Kat at her thirtieth birthday party. Certain memories should be like oil and water and never merge, yet they did, a hideous crossing over that left him feeling schizophrenic. He'd never quite learned to compartmentalize his thoughts. But the more horrors he witnessed, the more he knew he was right to let love in. Horror made love difficult to comprehend at times, leaching its colour, dampening its music, sapping its energy, but ultimately, he knew love couldn't be touched.

25

Hours of agony fell through Orla as she shuffled about the van's loadspace. Folded up within her legs, wrists cross-cuffed to her ankles, locked in a suffocating crash position, she was in a constant fight for breath, impossible to inhale fully with a crushed stomach. Her limbs, heavy and numb and useless, fizzed with paraesthesia. Righting herself from a fall took a harrowing amount of time and effort. She heard a passing car, footsteps, voices, even what sounded like a sniffing dog, and she called for help but no one came. No one out there to help her. Yet this was nothing compared to the pulsing agony of the promises she'd broken to her family. She shouted until her voice went and then let herself fall. She lay contorted in the dark and shut her eyes and wet herself.

Some interminable time later the sound of an engine. She rocked momentum into herself and got upright using her shoulders and knees, her knuckles, and she squatted there in the middle of the van, head following the sound of the engine and the gravel under the tyres. The car pulled up behind the van with its headlights on. An outline of white light marked out the double doors as if someone were burning through with a cutting torch. The engine idled but there was no movement. Just that thin edging of light. Then the engine cut and a door opened. Footsteps. Then nothing. Then more footsteps. Then one of the van's rear doors opening.

She squinted and turned her face from the headlight glaring behind the hooded figure. It stood there looking at her. Then it climbed in and walked stooped around her, slowly circling. It took down the hood of its parka. A big black guy she'd not seen before pushed her over and then kicked her along the floor of the van until she fell out, dropping to the rear step before hitting the ground.

She lay winded between van and car, a silver Mercedes, its chrome grille bearing down. He dropped out of the van and stood over her and switched on a powerful LED penlight and shone it in her face, turned, looked around. He pointed the light down the road, at the derelict house, and then into the van. He got out a phone and tapped the screen, his face glowing. He tapped the screen again and then lowered the phone and pointed the light at the van's plate, looked at the phone, looked at the plate. Then he looked at her. He rolled her on to her back and frisked her.

'What are you doing? Who are you? Please, help me.'

'You killed one of my boys. He was a father.'

'What? I haven't killed anyone.'

'Jem. Name ring a bell?'

The gypsy. Then this was Egan.

'How's that my fault? What did I do?'

'What did you do?' He rose. 'You made mistakes is what you did. Leaving your van on the moors when you went sniffing around the shooting box is what you did. Insuring that van under your home address is what you did. Taking the money back off my boy is what you did. Cutting his fucking throat is what you did. You want me to walk you through your other mistakes that led you to this moment?'

She lay there sick and silent and it dawned on her that she'd seen this car when she was driving home from the moors. Besides the small fleet at the shooting box, she'd seen two cars on the moors that night. A red BMW and a silver Mercedes. This silver Mercedes.

He moved towards the house and then stopped and looked at the van, at her, at the road, the fields, the trees, even the night sky. The blue-white beam of his penlight dancing madly over all it touched. He stepped into the van's loadspace and lifted things, moved them, threw them around, and when he stepped out he was carrying the shovel. He stood it leaning against the front tyre and then sat in the driver seat and looked about and a moment later he got back out and knelt and swept light under the van. He went to the house and tried the door handle. It didn't budge. He slammed into it with his shoulder. Nothing. He tried repeatedly until it gave and swung inward. Standing on the steps before entering the house, he turned and shone the penlight full in her face and then over the grounds, the fields, the road. He entered the house and went room to room, light flashing through slatted planks nailed across unglazed window frames.

She looked wild-eyed through the dark and heaved herself to her feet. She was waddling towards the trees, chin too close to her knees, when from behind, from the Mercedes, came the crackling of a two-way radio and a woman telling Egan to pick up. He came stomping back down the stairs and Orla sped up. He left the house, remotely opening the Mercedes's boot, and approached her. She'd almost reached the shelter of a thornbush and for a moment he stood watching her Sisyphean struggle as if it were some freakshow attraction, and then set his boot on her shoulder and toppled her. When she saw the Stanley knife in his fist, she heard herself whimper. He thumbed out the blade and pressed his knee into the side of her head, crushing her face into the ground.

'Where's my money?'

'They have it.'

'Where's my money?'

'Listen to me. The brothers have it.'

'What brothers?'

'The...' She couldn't remember the name. Then she could. 'Banskin. The Banskin brothers.'

He just stared at her.

'And Sweet,' she said. 'Millar Sweet. He said they're playing you. They're all laughing at you. They have your money.'

He seemed to consider this. Then he said: 'Where's my money?' He held the razor blade to her face. 'Tell me or I'm taking your ears.'

'Listen to me. They're all laughing—'

He pulled her ear out from her head and carved it off in three deep slices. She shrieked and tried rocking the pain and shock out of her system but his bulk was too much. He rolled her on to her back and covered her mouth with his hand. She moaned into his palm while he squinted through the dark for prying eyes.

'Your other ear's next.' He held the dripping cartilage over her face. 'Now where's my fucking money?'

24

The scaffolded country house and then Orla's van parked alongside the house appeared in the xenon burn of Sweet's headlights. Birds took off in fright of the lights and the roaring engine. He pulled up behind the van and saw its doors hanging open. His headlights partially filled the van's loadspace and lit the bulkhead. He sat looking out the windows. No movement. He got a flashlight from the glovebox and the Beretta from under his seat and shut off the engine, leaving the headlights glaring into the hollow of the van. He stepped warily from the Jaguar, eyes darting everywhere, ears tuning to many frequencies.

A cold wind. Smell of damp grass and pulled roots. The forlorn call of a nightbird. He switched on the flashlight and followed its beam to the boarded-up house. From the wide stone steps he looked inside the forced-open door and listened. The wind moved through leaves and grass with a sound like whispering. He looked up at the windows and aimed the light between the planks, into the black beyond. He moved back towards the van and turned on the spot, shining the light across the ground. Tyre tracks. He looked at the van's tracks and then moved behind the Jaguar and looked at its tracks. These tracks belonged to neither.

He circled the van, looked inside. Empty darkness. He went around the back of the house to an overrun wildflower garden bordered by a collapsed brick wall and looked out over it to the fields of high grass swaying bluely in the moonlight. An owl dropped silently from the sky and vanished into the grass. He returned to his car and was tapping the butt of the flashlight against the Jaguar's boot when he saw it. He squatted and focused the light. Like a scrawny rasher, pink and raw and spread in blood, a severed human ear crawling with ants.

He sped off in the same direction as the new tyre tracks. His phone rang. His father returning his update call. He answered and his father said without preface, his voice booming though the car's speakers: 'Who the fuck are the Banskin brothers?'

'Irrelevant.' Sweet ate a jelly baby. 'There's something else.'

'What?'

'The ferryman's out here.'

'What does that mean? Egan? Ah, fuck.' Something smashed.

'You want them putting down?'

'Guess.'

'All of them? That's…' Orla, Cy, Egan, the Banskins. 'Five.'

'So?'

'So nothing. However, it would appear my fee has risen considerably.' Sweet heard his mother's voice in the background and his lips peeled back in disgust. 'What does that cunt want?'

23

Orla lay doubled and bleeding in the boot of Egan's Mercedes. A claustral vacuum. The panic attacks came and went in waves, swinging her violently between nausea and horror. She was on the verge of blacking out and without light to wake up to, to focus on, she wasn't entirely sure she hadn't already. She tried to ignore the close heat and the blindness and the blaring pain in her ear and to concentrate on her breathing, on the road below her, on imagining the cold night wind on her face, but the slicing sound of her ear-lopping resonated.

The belief that she'd see her husband and daughter again gave her the strength to endure this airless hell, yet a repulsive foreboding slid through her and it told her this hell was heaven compared to the walk she must make across the floor of the pit, that benighted hole from where her family watched her with hatred in their eyes and bitterness in their hearts.

The car came to a stop and the engine cut. She was trying to hold her panting breath so she could hear him talk to the woman on the two-way radio, and though their words were unclear, the tone was calm, intimate. The car rocked as he got out. Approaching footsteps. She braced herself when the boot opened. He leaned in and grabbed her head in both hands and lifted it, bending and pressing her neck over the rim of the boot, twisting her head about as he presented to her the low drystone wall and the sloped cemetery beyond.

'This it?'

She tried to say 'I think so' but only a croak came out. He rattled her head and loosened a voice confirming it was. He scooped out her scrunched-up body, turned, let her go. She hit the ground hard, breathless and hurting yet more. He smelled his hands and pulled a face.

'Have you pissed yourself?'

He didn't wait for an answer, just wiped his hands on her shoulders. He took out a pistol and the penlight and switched on the light and bit it between his front teeth and then squatted beside her and held the muzzle of the pistol to the chain between one of the sets of cuffs, averted his face and pulled the trigger. A bright muzzle flash, a violent recoil, a rolling report echoing outward in every direction. Her left foot and right hand were free. He repeated the process, freeing her right foot and left hand, and then he stepped back and pointed the pistol at her face.

'Get up.'

She slowly uncurled on the ground, her first deep inhalation in hours filling her up, cool air billowing through her. She rose juddering, arms and legs dead, back muscles cramped up, circulatory system haywire. She crumpled against the wall in a tangle of thistles and then used the wall to get vertical. Finally straightened out, she looked at the silver bracelets ringing her wrists and ankles. Then she vomited. He took her shovel out of the boot and thrust it into her chest.

'Take me to it.'

She stood there pressing a hand to the side of her head and looking at the red on her fingers. 'I need a doctor.'

'You need to walk.'

She was struggling over the drystone wall when he pressed the pistol into the base of her skull.

'Should I threaten you? Should I explain that if you tried anything, I'd bend you over and stick this gun up you and pull the trigger and leave you to die out here? Should I mention these things?'

'No.'

'Kick off your boots.'

She looked down at her boots and then looked back up. 'Why?'

'You've done enough running. Kick 'em off.'

She took off the boots and stood there holding them.

136

'Put them on the wall.'

She set them on the wall.

'And the socks.'

She took off the socks.

'Put one in each boot.'

She put one in each boot.

'Now walk.'

She veered barefoot on legs of rubber. Grass blades cold and stiff between her toes, sharp. When her knees shuddered and buckled, she'd drop the shovel and cling to gravestones and then continue ascending the cemetery hill, rising towards the great oak. She looked behind to see him right there, pistol held in both hands pointing at the back of her head.

Even without her boots or socks she still considered running, attacking, even playing dead, but now they were at the top of the cemetery, beside the grave of Mildred Hobbs, and she gave up the fight. She'd been fighting all her life and was no further down the road than she'd ever been. She was destined for a life of subjugation. And she was hurting and more exhausted than she thought possible.

'This it?'

'Yeah.'

'Dig.'

The soil was wet with rain, waterlogged, sloppy, sliding off the shovel, the digging relatively easy, but still she dug slowly, as if to delay the inevitable handover. He stood behind the gravestone, facing the motorway downhill, the pistol trained on her at all times. Soon the blade hit the case and she saw a streak of orange in the dirt. She looked up.

'Look, I've done what you said. How about we split—'

He spat in her face. 'Dig.'

137

She wiped the spit and shifted the soil from around the edges of the case and reached in and lifted it out by its handle. Kneeling in the grass, she held on to the case with her head lowered and her eyes shut. She didn't think she could let go. It was beyond money. This was something more. This was pride. Easier failing than quitting. But she did let go. She offered up the case in both hands and the world she'd built in her skull, a stable future of deep roots and solid foundations, a world of immunity and choice, that world vanished.

She looked up at Egan, balancing the case on the gravestone, and then she shut her eyes and hung her head, a flabby echo of blood gurgling along her ear canal, somewhere behind her eye. The physical pain of only minutes ago now meant nothing. It barely registered as she sank deeper, reverting to a cold state of despair that had frozen her life solid for too many years. She wasn't a person. She was a pietà sculpture. The sound of the pistol slide pulling back woke her.

'Wait. There has to be something. Please.' She was looking at the case. She was unable to take her eyes from it. 'There has to be…we can work something out. Come on. I did everything you said.'

'Your bitch and baby didn't whine this much.'

She blanched through her sweat.

'I visited them, and after you're gone, I'm going back. Do you understand what I'm telling you?'

The night rang in her ears and something inside her cracked and fell away and all that was left was her family. She was slammed violently between rage and despair.

'Oh, god. Tell me they're okay. Just tell me they're okay.' She wiped tears and dirt and snot and blood from her face. 'You fucking…tell me you haven't hurt them. If you've hurt them…'

She saw herself beside Liam in bed and the baby lying between them, gazing up, her lenses learning to focus in the dark, her hands reaching, holding on to Orla's thumb. But the image was a sneering joke, now emetic to her, poison, and was disgorged in a fierce, howling moan.

'You'll be with them soon enough.' Egan unlatched the case and looked inside. Then he frowned, opening the case further. 'What the fuck?'

The quaking crack of a gunshot from the lane and a hot wash broke against her face and arms. She fell back and lay in the grass, looking up at him. Half his head and face blown out. Flesh and bone grotesquely flowered in a gory bloom. A red cloud hung in the air at the back of his head. Then he bent at the waist and folded over the gravestone and the case fell back into the hole. Blood dripped down the stone and collected in Mildred Hobbs's name, in the year of her birth, in the year of her death, in the flatline dash between that was her life.

Orla dropped on to her stomach in the grass and looked through the gravestones to the lane and saw Egan's Mercedes. The driver-side door hung open. Maybe it had been open before, she couldn't remember. But now there was another car out there. A Jaguar. Then she saw that eerily boyish stranger with the smooth skin and the slicked-back silvery hair. He was in the cemetery, carrying a scoped rifle and searching at his feet for something. He bent to retrieve whatever it was and dropped it into his trouser pocket. Then he came forward, rifle hanging at his waist.

Still on her belly she reached down into the hole and lifted the case and set it on the grass. Some of the money had fallen out and she reached back into the world below and retrieved as much as she could, stuffing dirtied bundles into the case and locking it. Three bundles still down there. She considered the risk, decided against it, and instead took Egan's pistol from the grass and his keys from his parka and fled downhill in the opposite direction to Sweet, crouched low, keeping to the gravestones. Hunched behind a slab of black marble with her back to its cold face, the sound of her heart and the world in one ear, the other plugged mute with coagulate blood.

She looked back up the hill. Sweet was anatomizing Egan's corpse, prodding the open head wound with something, maybe a pen or a pencil. She wiped her forearm over her dripping face and moved on, changing direction again, now moving towards the drystone wall, towards the cars. She waited for Sweet to look away before jumping the wall. She landed hard on the other side in the gravel on her unshod feet but they were numb with something more than cold and she felt nothing. Sitting in the lane in a growth of nettles and hogweed, back to the wall, case in her lap. She saw her boots on the wall past the cars but couldn't risk it. She looked up at the black mantle of sky overflowing with stars. Then she ran.

She threw the case and the gun inside the Mercedes and sat low in the driver seat. The top of the wall at eye level. Sweet stood appraising the dark land through the rifle scope. When he turned away, she shut the door, not fully, just enough so it wouldn't swing open again. He'd moved further downhill now, sweeping the rifle through the dark. A silent flash of light and then the burst of a gunshot and the wall's mossed coping exploded beside her head, debris hitting the window, glass vibrating with resistance, thunder resounding through the car. She pushed the engine button. Nothing happened. She'd never driven a car like this. She frantically mashed the button while stepping barefoot on the pedals and finally it came alive. Accelerating, hurtling towards the motorway. Another shot from behind and a long streak of light crossed the bonnet as the bullet struck at a shallow angle and echoed into the hedgerow. Another shot rang but she'd rounded the curve and was merging with the night traffic on the motorway.

22

Sweet looked through the scope of the rifle, forefinger on the trigger, watching the Mercedes weave through the lanes until it vanished from sight. Only then did he lower the rifle. He looked about his feet and collected the spent shells from the grass and dropped them in his pocket along with the one that had contained the hollow-point bullet now in pieces in Egan's erupted skull. He estimated the distances between himself and the Jaguar and the Mercedes and committed them to memory to commit to his notebook. He walked back uphill and squatted at the open grave of Mildred Hobbs and looked again at Egan bent over the headstone, gaped skull dripping and steaming in the cold. He saw the bundles of money down in the hole and he knelt and reached and picked them out and flicked through them and put them in his jacket pocket and took out his notebook and wrote something down. He pushed Egan's corpse to the grass and rolled it behind the gravestone, tucking the limbs away, out of sight from the motorway and the single-track road. He went downhill and turned and looked back at the grave. Nothing out of the ordinary. He walked towards the Jaguar and looked back. It was as if nothing had happened. He noted the brand and size of the boots on the wall and then climbed over the wall and stood in the middle of the lane beside the Jaguar, still wielding the rifle at his hip, studying the acres outspread before him. Satisfied, he opened the boot and lifted the carpeted floor panel and set the rifle in the empty and widened spare-tyre well and then sat in the car and took methylphenidate and wrote in his notebook. Equations and technical diagrams, lists and calculations, estimations and theories. He didn't notice the headlights go out behind him.

21

The trees fell away and the gravestones rose over the wall. They were back at the cemetery where Orla McCabe had given them the slip. Joseph touched the brake and slowed Tolmach's van to a crawl. They were looking for the break in the wall that opened into the cemetery, the place where Orla McCabe had been about to turn in. The lane curved and Joseph drifted into the bend, and as the lane straightened, he saw the parked car. A Jaguar. He shut off his headlights and swung the van next to a ditch in the hedgerow.

They sat very still. Watching. The interior light was on in the Jaguar and a figure was moving about inside. They got out, leaving their doors open, and flanked the Jaguar in broad, soundless arcs. Joseph through the hedgerow, Dolan jumping the wall and running crouched along its length inside the cemetery. When he was parallel with the Jaguar, Dolan took the chisel-point knife from his pocket and leapt the wall and reached in through the window, pressing the blade against the skin below Sweet's eye.

'Move and you're blind.'

Joseph emerged from the hedgerow and opened the rear door, slid along the back seat, hooked the sickle around Sweet's neck and pulled his head back into the headrest with the blade. Dolan went around the Jaguar to join Joseph in the back.

'Take out the key and turn out the light.'

Sweet eyed them in the rear-view and then did as he was told.

'You killed my uncle.'

'Who's your uncle?'

'Cy Green.'

Joseph thought about this and nodded. 'We killed your uncle.'

Sweet gripped the wheel and his jaw clenched, a muscle jumping in his throat. 'I know where she is. I know where she is and I know where the money is.'

'You don't.'

'I can take you to her. You could live like kings. You could live like me.'

Dolan unravelled the bandage from around his head and looked over Sweet's shoulder into the rear-view. The black plectrum of his sheared nose resembled that of a bat. He turned his head this way and that, inspecting the wound, and then reapplied the bandage.

'Those boots out there, they hers?'

'That's my assumption,' Sweet said.

'Who's Henry?'

'Henry? He's my cousin. Cy's son. Why?'

'Enough.' Joseph pressed his hand flat to the back of Sweet's headrest and readjusted his grip on the sickle handle.

Sweet's hand rose viperous, gripping a small PAVA spray canister taken from his belt and a thin jet of liquid hit Joseph in the face. Joseph reeled back and the blade bit deeper into Sweet's throat before Joseph let go, dropping the sickle. Tears streamed,

143

burning light from his eyes. His respiratory system toxically scorched. Dolan lunged at Sweet but he was too quick. He'd sprung from the car and was training the Beretta on them through the side window, his other hand holding his split throat, blood leaking through his fingers.

'Out.' Sweet spoke through his teeth. 'Get the fuck out of my car.'

They stepped out and Sweet blasted them with the spray. Snot and drool and tears pouring through their hands.

He pointed the gun at Joseph. 'Get on your knees. You, on your fucking knees.'

Joseph fell slowly to his knees, inflamed eyes flooded.

'Put your hands behind your head and your forehead on the ground.'

Joseph did as he was told while coughing and retching.

'Move a muscle and I put a bullet in your head. You hear me, you fucking freak?' Sweet turned the gun on Dolan. 'You, around the back.'

Dolan went to the back of the Jaguar.

Sweet opened the boot. 'Get in.'

Dolan just stood there, holding his streaming face.

'I said get the fuck in.' Sweet let go of his dribbling throat long enough to grab Dolan by his scruff and push him in. Then he sidestepped, never taking the gun off Dolan, and kicked Joseph in the head.

'Now you, fucko. Up.'

Joseph rose and stood at full height, towering over Sweet.

'In the boot, now.'

Blinded, Joseph felt his way around the back of the Jaguar. Then, in a sudden movement, he pivoted. But Sweet was fast. The gunshot took apart Joseph's knee and instantly felled him.

'Next bullet will be in your brother's face. Right in that arsehole where his nose was. Now get in.'

Joseph struggled to his feet and then contorted himself into the boot. By the time he was finished, Dolan could barely be seen.

'Now toss the shivs.'

They didn't move.

Sweet drew a stun gun that resembled a curved electric shaver and gave them a few volts. They convulsed and gargled, faces straining purple. He told them again, and after much effort some rusted and oddly shaped knives were cast to the ground. Sweet slammed darkness into the boot.

The handkerchief he now held to his throat had turned red and was dripping and sagging with the weight of blood. He got in the car and leaned up and forward to see his slit throat in the rearview and pounded the wheel, disgusted at himself for allowing this to happen. He drove erratically through unlit wooded paths, hitting dips and deep muddy ruts and several times grounding the car. More than once he had to jump on the brake and swing the wheel when a tree or a bend in the road appeared in the white cones of the headlights.

At some point during the mayhem of the journey, sensing something behind him, he pulled up and looked around, turning his entire upper body, afraid of opening up the shallow cut in his throat that was slowly clotting. Wriggling fingers were reaching through the ski hatch in the back seat.

'Listen up, lads,' he called. 'I know you can hear me, so listen up. I was going to kill you quick. I was going to put one in your head and you wouldn't have felt a thing, but now you're going to feel it, now you're going to feel everything. You hear me? Our mutual friend's going to make sure of that. You've got a big surprise coming to you.'

He jabbed the hand with the stun gun and it contracted and vanished back down the hatch. Eerily the bottled spiders made no sound. Neither when shot nor shocked.

20

After finding loose change and a roll of hundreds in the armrest compartment of Egan's Mercedes, Orla stopped at a supermarket on her way home and parked near the entrance. She considered going in herself but the pandemonium of pain in her head and the commotion she'd doubtlessly cause, barefoot and missing an ear, forced her hand. So she waited. Drowsy and sick and bitter cold, she waited.

A roadworker walked by wearing steel-toe boots, an orange high-vis jacket and a hard hat. He was about twenty-five and covered in dirt. She called out to him. He looked around, apprehensive, and then moved cautiously towards the Mercedes.

'Could you do me a favour? Could you get me a first-aid kit?' She turned her head to show her mutilation. 'I'll pay you.' She held out two fifties of Egan's money.

'What happened?'

'I was attacked.'

'I'll call the police.' He reached into his pocket but she stopped him.

'Please.' She thrust the money at him.

He hesitated and then said, 'Yeah, okay,' and took the money.

'And some painkillers. Strongest they have.'

'Okay.'

'Listen, they took my boots as well.'

'Your boots?'

'And socks.'

He cautiously leaned forward to look. 'Jesus. You need to call the police. What size?'

She watched him disappear inside the supermarket and then slid into concussive sleep. In the dream she saw Liam and their daughter sprawled cold and naked on a blue hilltop, their bone-white skin writhen with the shadows of circling birds, and in this dream their daughter was older and she could talk but when she opened her mouth to say something, her head started to tremble and split open. Orla woke in fright and looked at the clock. A minute hadn't passed.

The roadworker came back carrying two shopping bags. He tapped on the glass and she had to concentrate to find the button to lower the window. He handed her the bags.

'I got you some water and sandwiches too. The money's in there. It's on me.'

She didn't know what to say.

'Good luck,' he said.

She nodded dumbly and started the engine, watching him in the rear-view as she drove off. He was watching her too. She circled around and pulled up alongside him as he was getting into his car.

'I couldn't use your phone, could I?'

She parked up a little away from his car and got out and went barefoot across to him. He looked her over as he handed her the phone. She paced about the Mercedes in the car park, listening to her landline phone ring. Finally Liam answered.

'Liam, are you hurt, is the baby okay?' She stood rock-still even as the chill of the ground rose into the floors of her feet.

'You said you were coming home.' His voice was different somehow, decelerated and slurred, as if his jaws had been wired shut. 'You promised.'

'I know but…I couldn't. These people.' The darkness of Egan's words eclipsed the relief at hearing his voice. 'Did he hurt you?'

'You promised.'

'I'm on my way.' Tears formed and she let them spill. 'I'm on my way. I miss you both so much.'

'She won't settle.' His voice almost inaudible. 'She keeps crying for you. Orla, she won't stop crying.'

'I'm sorry for putting you through this. I'm so sorry.' Guilt hardened around her, walling her in. 'You've got to forgive me.'

His silence lay on her like a mountain.

Finally he said: 'Just come home.'

19

Heat and darkness and the muffled babble of voices. Then the boot opened and light swept in. The silhouettes of Sweet and Tolmach loomed overhead, looking down into the space where Dolan and Joseph lay folded in turmoil, bleeding and suffocating, eyes gushing. Sweet held the Beretta in one hand and the PAVA canister in the other. A bandage had been taped around his throat. Tolmach held a rag and a brown medicine bottle, flashlight bit between his front teeth. Sweet sprayed Joseph's face and eyes and then pulled the bandage from around Dolan's head and gave him the same. While the captives retched and choked and held their faces, Tolmach doused the rag and pressed it over Joseph's mouth and nose, gripping his entire face and bouncing his head off the floor of the boot. It took a while for him to stay down. He doused the rag again, leaned over Joseph's unconscious bulk, and did the same to Dolan. Oblivion's blackness flooded their brains and shut them down.

Cold water broke against Dolan's face and he came to. He shook the water from his hair and beard and coughed hard. Snot and blood bubbling in his frayed nose hole. His eyes stung and continually wept. He'd been roped to a two-wheel hand truck and stood upright.

Tolmach backed up and threw a steel bucket against the stable wall and sat heavily on a three-legged milking stool. He was drunk and sweaty and out of breath, eyes half shut, looking ready to pass out. He picked up a bottle of whisky and knocked back a deep swig and set the bottle down, kicked out his leg and placed both hands on his outstretched knee, head fallen at a sharp angle.

Sweet stood in the stable entrance near the skidsteer loader, dry-swallowing pills and smoothing back his hair. He touched the bandage around his throat and when he noticed Dolan had come to, he turned fully to watch.

'Your kin's sleeping off his gelding,' Tolmach said. 'He put up a fight. Just like the old days.'

Dolan looked to his side. Joseph was standing beside him, lashed to another upright hand truck, his slumped head fitted with a rope hackamore like a scold's bridle. His fallen wet hair quivered on the breeze of a faint breath. He was naked from the waist down, his legs awash with blood. On the concrete at his feet lay gobs of stringy red-white meat in oily puddles of their own juices.

'He'll live,' Tolmach said. 'Least long enough to wake up in there.' He pointed over his shoulder with a knife to the two pine-box coffins that lay in the grass outside the stable and then put the knife in his pocket and picked up the whisky bottle, finished the dregs and slammed the bottle against Dolan's head three, four times. The bottle didn't break, so instead Tolmach pushed his thumb into Dolan's nose hole and then went behind him and tipped over the hand truck. Without a nose to bear the brunt, Dolan's brow ridge struck the hurtling concrete with a wet crack.

From the edges of a bleary eye Dolan watched Tolmach wheel Joseph outside, untie him from the hand truck and shake him loose. His hands still tied behind his back, Joseph fell headlong into one of the coffins. Tolmach walked around the coffin, tucking in Joseph's legs, and then he came back into the stable. Dolan tried to lift his face from the concrete but could not. He heard back-and-forth movement, shuffling, something dragging across concrete—no idea what was happening. Then the floor pulled away and he was upright again and being wheeled past the skid-steer and out of the stable into a curtain of cold rain. He was stood beside the coffins under the dead pear tree.

Sweet walked away talking on his phone, back to his Jaguar parked over in the courtyard.

Tolmach fitted the lid on Joseph's coffin and then went about it, hammering it shut with long nails from his pocket. In his drunken stupor he missed many times and caught his thumb. He swore and pounded the lid with the hammer. Sucking his thumb, he finished the job one-handed. The hole in the ground at the head of Joseph's coffin had no length but was very deep. Then Dolan saw why. Tolmach pushed the coffin from the end where Joseph's feet lay until his head was somewhere over the hole and then began lifting at the feet end. It took great effort, especially

150

bladdered, but soon gravity took over and the coffin upended, rising vertically into the air like a sinking ship, and Joseph slid boxed-up inside the coffin down into the earth.

Tolmach stood swaying over the hole, laughing as he unzipped his boilersuit and shrugged out of its top half and pissed on the coffin. He zipped up and tried stepping over the hole but tripped, losing a leg down there, but the hole, now Joseph's coffin had filled it, lay barely a foot deep. He stepped back out, still laughing to himself. The laughter collapsed into a moan and rose into an agonized howl. He leaned and vomited on the dirt pile he'd taken out of the ground. Then he picked up a shovel and filled the hole. When he finished he threw the shovel into the grass and held his hips, trying to orient himself. He looked at Dolan.

'You're up.'

He undid the ropes that kept Dolan lashed to the hand truck but not the ropes around his arms and torso that tied his hands behind his back. He pushed him between his shoulders and Dolan crashed into his pine box. He twisted until he'd turned himself on to his back, lying on his bound hands, looking up at the overhanging branches of the pear tree and the black sky spilling rain.

Tolmach appeared overhead, carrying a glass tank under one arm. He climbed on top of the coffin and stood with his legs wide apart on the lengthwise edging.

'Rose's wee boy was dug up in the commune a few years back in a box just like yours. Remember that? Wee thing'd been buried alive. They found him with his knees drawn up to his chin and his clothes all ripped up. His fingernails wrecked. He'd pulled out most of his hair and bit off his tongue. The walls of his world had closed in. I can't imagine a more perfect horror.' He smiled and reached into the tank. 'Except maybe this.'

He held by a gangly foreleg the giant huntsman spider. Legs cycling frictionless, the spider shuddered and contracted as if trying to curl itself into a fist. Tolmach's grin hung askew but was soon wiped when the spider righted itself and seized his hand. He cried out and shook his whole arm. In his panic he dropped the tank to the grass and his footing went, and he fell into the coffin beside Dolan.

Dolan headbutted him five, six, seven times and then leaned and bit his face, worrying it, chewing skin and muscle, chomping down on jaw and cheekbone. He pressed his face into his throat. Horrible gargling moans and then Tolmach fell mute, his sputum-coloured eyes glassing over.

With a sopping beard, Dolan emerged from the bloody swamp of Tolmach's neck. He looked down the length of his own body and watched the spider heave itself up over his boots and out of the coffin. He rolled on to his side, turning his back on Tolmach, and groped behind himself for the knife in the old man's boiler-suit pocket. Many long minutes of blind fumbling passed before he found it and cut his hands free.

He lay listening for Sweet. All he heard was wind, rain, a bird call. He rose from the coffin and looked down at Tolmach. His blood filling the pine floor. He looked at the dirt-filled hole where Joseph stood castrated on his bridled head and he looked at the shovel in the grass. He turned to the Jaguar parked across the field in the mired courtyard outside the farmhouse.

Wielding Tolmach's knife, he moved towards the Jaguar. He hunkered behind a rotted fence covered in snails and watched Sweet through the open driver-side window, head tipped back looking in the rear-view at the bandage around his throat, touching bloodstains that had clouded up with one hand, holding a phone to his ear with the other.

'No, these banknotes are in pounds sterling,' he said. 'Of course I'm sure. Well, in that case we have a problem. No, that wasn't a pun.'

Dolan rushed forward and swung the knife through the open window into Sweet's face. Sweet gave an odd sneeze from one nostril and Dolan pulled out the knife and cut his throat and then reached through the window and retrieved the fallen phone and listened.

'Millar?' A man's voice. 'Millar, are you there? Answer me. Fuck.'

The line clicked dead.

He pocketed the phone and left Sweet where he lay and went back to the burial site and dug out the soil over Joseph's coffin. His shot arm meant digging was slow and gruelling. Rainworms writhed in knotty clusters in the sodden earth. He knocked on the pine top with the shovel. He called to Joseph. No answer. He went around the back of the farmhouse.

A talismanic horseshoe hung on the toolshed door. He entered the dank gloom. On the dusty concrete floor beside a sawhorse lay a hickory-haft axe. He picked it up and looked around. Took a crowbar suspended from a nail pounded through the masonry. Before leaving he found the rest of his and Joseph's clothes in a pile on the floor. Joseph's stolen rings and the photos he'd taken from Orla McCabe's home and her driving licence lay on a scarred workbench beside a vice. He took the rings and the photos and the licence and pulled on his poncho.

He chopped a hole through the pine board, wrenched it off with the crowbar and reached in through the splinters. One arm lost in the afterworld, the rest of his body in this. He gripped Joseph's ankle. Nothing. No heat, no movement. Cold rain trickled down his ear and into the brain-warmed dark of his head. He levered off the end board from his own coffin, releasing Tolmach's blood in a thick overspill, and laid the board over Joseph's roof-less chamber. He filled in the hole and then trudged cold and draggled about the quaggy field and neighbouring wood collecting large stones and he built a finely balanced cairn upon his brother's oubliette.

In the farmhouse kitchen, he drank four cups of water and then went back to the Jaguar, the cold water gulping and rolling in his stomach as he bent to pull Sweet's corpse out. He dropped the bled carcass to the rain-dappled mud and turned out its pockets, retrieved a notebook, a pencil, three bundles of money and a Beretta. He sat in the car, the leather wet with Sweet's cold piss and blood, and opened the notebook and read Sweet's thoughts in the ink on the page and in the blood on the glass.

From trees at the field's edge, Tolmach's blue-eyed horse stood watching Dolan. Surrounding the horse were four shadowed figures. One of the figures, a lank and hatted man, was stroking the animal's velvet nose. He emerged from the trees, bearded and wearing a filthy brown suit, bare-chested under the suit's buttoned-up jacket. His shuffling walk strange in tattered brogues too big for his feet. The laces tied around the shoes themselves and around his naked ankles to keep them on. He knocked back his preacher's hat with his knuckles and held out his arms cruciform, frayed jacket sleeves riding up to reveal tattooed symbols on his forearm, and as he neared their eyes met and his lips moved. Dolan couldn't hear what he was saying. The man passed Joseph's cairn and his eyes briefly lowered to take in the sight. His shadow reached back across the smoking grass to the place where his acolytes clustered. When the horse crumpled to its knees and Arden was close enough to be heard—*skin for skin, brother*—Dolan started the engine and fled that diabolic ground.

18

The little flat-bottomed skiff rocked and creaked as the river slid under its anchored weight. The skipper of that one-man vessel realigned the reel and leaned out over the gunwale where the weighted tube lights bordering the boat gave off an evil green nimbus as they pitched and dipped in the dark of the night depths. He reached into the tackle box and took out a can of super-strength lager and leaned back into the bow, cracking open the can and drinking, a cold flow of wind streaming across his face. Cloud had covered the moon and like the yoked bobbing lights, the moon pulsed through a swirl of cover with a deep glow. Out in the Irish Sea its horizon lay constellated with oil-rig gas flares and wandering ships and wind-farm warning lights. The taut line unspooling from the reel twanged and he opened his eyes and leaned forward. He checked the reel and adjusted the mounted floodlight, angling its beam into the water. Nothing. Silty murk. He set down his can and leaned out over the other side, hands on raw wood, paint flayed long ago. The black pointed shapes of fish darted within the green burn of the submerged lights. He was leaning back when an anaemic hand came into view, waving off rags of its own flesh like tissue paper. He rose and stepped back. The skiff swayed and the can tipped and rolled over the planking, lager chugging out. A ghostly heron standing mute in the shore reeds squatted from view and then slowly pushed itself up into the night, long legs stiffly dangling. He leaned over and looked again. The dark little fish had turned their limited attention to the hand like sperm penetrating some horribly imagined egg. He swore to himself as he pull-started the outboard motor with quaking hands.

17

Carlin read the report a second time.

The body of the man had been found by a night fisherman in a reed bed during the early hours. A preliminary forensic analysis had determined that the body had been in the water less than a week and that before immersion he'd been stabbed in his right carotid artery and strangled with such force his hyoid bone had fractured. According to his wallet he was sixty-four-year-old Cyrus Green. The same sixty-four-year-old Cyrus Green whose name was on the deeds to the moorland shooting box. The last GPS coordinates issued by his phone before it had been powered down or its battery had died pointed to an isolated farmstead a few hours' drive north-east.

Lynch came into the office carrying his phone and a coffee, a document folder under his arm. Carlin handed him the report and finished his morning tea and then stood up, putting on his coat.

Lynch read the report. 'Have you called his family?'

'I tried to speak to his wife but his son came on the line, Henry, ranting and raving, saying if we don't find who did this, he will. He was quite emphatic.'

The farmstead was cordoned off and a helicopter hovered in the rain. Lynch and Carlin moved among the bodies in silence, neither speculating on what had happened in that barren and secluded wasteland. Animal bones strewn about the fields, dog and horse skulls, ribcages, some recently burned. The fresh carcass of a blue-eyed horse lay in the trees, its throat slit, tail and penis lopped and missing.

They moved through the putrid farmhouse, pausing in each

room to take in the decay and the ruin and the sadness. Lynch looked at the mahogany acoustic guitar in pieces on the kitchen floor. Carlin stood before a greasy window overlooking the fields where uniformed officers were performing a fingertip search of the toolshed. The helicopter came in low and rattled the windows in their rotted frames. In a room off the kitchen, they looked on a wickedness that would ever echo through the mazy halls of their minds.

They stood in the courtyard beside the body of a young grey-haired man lying face down in the mud. He had a deep facial stab wound and his throat had been slashed. Across the field, under a dead pear tree, a group of forensics lingered over two pine-box coffins. One newly disinterred and stained with dirt. A man lay dead in each. One bitten and bled out. The other, a bearded giant wearing a horse bridle strapped to his head, bound, kneecapped and castrated.

They took a slow walk across the field through the wind and the rain and stopped to look at the two hand trucks, the empty glass tank, the muddy footprints. Based on a photo found in the house, the coffined old man with the chewed-up throat was the owner of the farm. Neither the neutered giant nor the slashed-up man in the mud had ID. The two detectives stood silhouetted in the stable doorway beside a skidsteer loader fitted with a dirt-covered auger. The stalls horseless. Horrible cuts of meat on the floor. Lynch wondered aloud what exactly the meat was and then realized and said no more. The helicopter moved in low and he looked up, watching its blades thrash the treetops. Then it was ascending, banking, moving off. Carlin looked ready to speak when a horrified yell tore open the silence. Someone had found what lived in the tank.

In the car on the way back to the station, Carlin asked for Lynch's opinion. Lynch shrugged and sighed, said something about evil. Carlin pushed him for theories, intentions, motivations, connections. He said using evil as the primary cause was a cop-out.

'Evil threads history together,' Lynch said. 'There's only evil. It's our gift to the world.'

'No. There has to be more.'

Lynch was silent for a while. Then he said: 'Why did they eat from the tree?'

'What are you talking about?'

But Lynch was watching the rain clouds. 'Let's just wait for the coroner's report.'

16

The boots the roadworker had bought her were cheap and made of fake leather and too small, but Orla's feet were numb and badly blistered. Better than nothing. She was parked off a country road in a chilly, dank corridor of trees. She disinfected and dressed her raw earhole, winding a bandage over her head and under her jaw like a chinstrap, and then took double the recommended dose of painkillers with the bottled water.

A loud bursting crackle and a female voice came through the two-way radio calling for Egan, telling him to pick up, and Orla jumped and cried out. The voice called again.

Orla picked up the radio and said: 'Orla McCabe is dead. Stop looking for her.'

A sustained pause and then the woman said: 'Who the fuck is this? Where's Egan? Put Egan—'

Orla tore out the radio wire and got out and leaned on the car with both hands, head hanging between her arms, muscle and bone pining for rest. She tried walking off the nightmare, back and forth around the car, through a black and mildewy rill of slimy dead leaves, cuff bracelets clinking about her feet like spurs. The skin of her wrists and ankles was lacerated and bruised. She pulled at the bracelets, bunching her fingers together, seeing if there was a chance of slipping out. Impossible without breaking a few bones. She pulled the sleeves of her jacket and the hems of her jeans down over the bracelets and looked at the rifle damage on the bonnet, touched the crude shooting-star logo left behind.

She sat in the car and ran her fingertips over the bright satanic millstone of the case. It was the terminator line separating day from night, want from need, all from nothing. While in possession of the case, she was in a state of superposition, both dead and alive, rich and poor. As were her family. She took out Sweet's business card from her pocket and Egan's gun from the glovebox, and contemplated them, and in the unmapped continents of her mind, a spark kindled an inferno and her baby girl appeared before her eyes to vindicate this lunacy. She put the gun in the case and the case in the boot and then drove off the country lane to the road. Out the passenger window the road tapered north from where she'd come. Out her window the road tapered south towards home. She finished the water and headed north. To the sea.

15

When Lynch and Carlin got back to the station, the Detective Chief Superintendent was waiting for them with news. Something had been recovered from the shot laptop taken from the shooting box. They were led to a room where three high-ranking officers and two National Crime Agency officers sat at desks facing a large TV.

The DCS and one of the NCA officers talked about the dark web and its markets for drugs and explosives, firearms and chemicals, computer viruses and passports, the personal data of millions, illegal pornography, organ trading, kill lists, animal cruelty, hit men. They talked of video livestreams in which people are tortured and executed at the whims of paying viewers. With these vices in mind, they speculated on what was happening at the shooting box. Then the lights were shut off and the blinds closed. They advised them to prepare themselves and then played a video livestreamed the year before.

When the video ended Lynch and Carlin went down to the drenched courtyard. Two groups of firearms officers were piling into vans and speeding out of the security gates. Beyond the station walls their sirens began. While Carlin lit a cigarette, Lynch went to the wall and leaned on the wet brickwork and spewed into a clogged gutter and wiped his hand across his mouth. His face was grey, his lips blue. Carlin looked up through the rain and smoked with an unsteady hand. Lynch looked him in the eye, stared at him, debating whether to tell him something. An airliner floated over, low and loud, heading south for the airport. Lynch swore and walked away, and Carlin dropped his cigarette and wiped rain from his eyes. He watched the young detective walk stiffly to his car and tear out of the courtyard.

Carlin bought vending-machine chicken soup on his way back up to his office. His hands still quaking as he moved down the corridors, he managed to scald himself with the boiling liquid. On his desk was a sealed envelope with his name handwritten across the back in red marker. In the envelope, a series of photos. Photos of his house. Photos of his car outside his house. Photos of his wife getting out of her car. Photos of his wife entering their house. He scattered the photos and the envelope across the room and then threw the door shut. He sat down and swallowed pills with a bottle of water. He looked at the photos lying there on the floor and he pounded the desk. Sweat ran from his thinned-out hair. He got out his phone and dialled a number.

'You send me photos of my home? Photos of my wife? Fuck you. Fuck. You. Go near my family or my home again and I'll break your fucking neck. Are you forgetting who I am? Oh, that's funny, is it? Right, okay. We'll see who laughs last.'

He hung up and threw the phone across the room. It came apart against a whiteboard covered in mugshots and surveillance photos, coloured handwriting and connecting arrows. A knock on the door and the door opened a crack. He said 'not now' without looking and the door shut. He caught his breath and picked up the photos and the pieces of his phone and sat back down, sliding the photos into the envelope, reassembling the phone.

The phone call to his creditor and the video they'd been shown noxiously merged and played in an endless loop in his mind. The laughter of his creditor playing over the heartbreaking sight of the doomed teen boy in the concrete chamber. Thoughts of suicide close, lately they were always close, always within reach, no effort required to conjure the welcoming void. It was the only thing in his life over which he had any power, but what power it was: The power to uncreate creation.

He put the envelope in his desk drawer and picked up his coat. Lynch's desk phone rang across the room. He headed for the door and stopped and looked out the window. He saw himself falling with the rain and hitting the ground, lying on his front in the courtyard with his head snapped around, looking up at the faces gawping down at him. Satisfaction at their horror. Welcome to my world, cunts. Lynch's phone was still ringing when he left the office.

14

Liam flushed the toilet and then struggled to wash his hand, the other loosely cradled in a sling made from a shirt. Since the attack he'd had an irrepressible palsy and found it impossible to get warm. His fingers and toes frozen to the touch. He left his hand under the blistering water until it turned red and the mirror over the sink steamed up and his beaten face became a blur in the glass. He panted as he shuffled down the stairs, using the banister and the wall for support. He was slowly descending when a figure in the front door's frosted glass pressed the doorbell.

He stopped and stared one-eyed at the figure. It didn't move. He went into the living room and looked out the window and saw a parked car and on the doorstep in the rain stood an attractive pale-skinned woman in her early forties. She wore a leather jacket and tight black jeans and black leather boots. Red lipstick. Long black hair brushed back into a tight ponytail. She knocked on the door and he looked at the baby in her basket and looked again at the woman. Then he opened the door.

She recoiled and covered her mouth with her hand when she saw his face. He just stood there, looking at her through one eye, the other eye sealed in a clammed purple dome, his swollen mouth the same colour.

'Oh, god. I was just…' She pointed vaguely over her shoulder. He noticed the wedding ring. 'I was just knocking to ask for directions. I'm lost. I'm not from around here.'

He held on to the jamb, shut his eye, opened it. He felt he could pass out.

'Are you okay?' She stepped forward and touched his arm.

'I'm fine. I'm…I have to go.' He started closing the door.

'Have you seen a doctor? Do you want me to call an ambulance?'

The baby started sobbing and Liam said he had to go and tried closing the door again.

'Let me help. I can help you.'

Tears brimmed in his eyes when she asked if he was alone with the baby.

'Why?'

'Because you look like you're about to drop and I can't walk away and leave that baby alone. I can't. I couldn't live with myself if I heard something had happened to you or the baby and I'd done nothing. I'll have to call the police or an ambulance.'

Too tired to resist, he relented and stood aside. She entered and he shut the door and followed her into the living room. Seeing him struggling, she held his elbows and lowered him on to the couch.

'I'll do you a drink. The kitchen through here?'

'Wait.' He gestured for the baby.

She picked up the basket by its arched handle and set it down on the couch beside him.

'I'm doing you a drink and then I'm calling an ambulance.'

'No, I'm fine, really.'

'You don't look fine.'

'I am.'

'At least let me take you to the hospital.'

'I'm okay.'

She sighed. 'I really wish you'd get looked at. You might have a concussion. Your hand's blue.'

'It's nothing.'

'How's the baby?'

'We're both okay.'

She opened the door to the kitchen and stopped, looking at the back door held shut with a dining chair. The door rattling in the wind, hanging untrue in its frame. Rain pooling under the chair rippled from a draught. She went back into the living room and sat on the couch beside him.

The baby started to cry.

'I'm not leaving you two alone until I know you're both safe.' She placed her hand on his knee. 'What happened?'

13

Lynch looked dead. He was sitting on the couch in his apartment with his hands palm up at his sides, slack-jawed, his eyes flat and vague. The cold light coming in from the balcony ran over the glass coffee table and then a cloud came along and the light dissolved. Silence. Expensive silence. Silence he'd paid for.

It was like a pressure, the air heavy with it, a solid presence with its own weight and mass pressing down on all sides.

The video he and Carlin had been shown ran vivid in his mind. He tried to shake the savagery and focus on the details, but it was difficult. The negative-space handprint tattoo between the shoulder blades of the masked man. As if paint had been blown over a hand splayed against his back. Like hand stencils in cave art. He couldn't imagine too many of those out there. The silence was shattered by his ringing phone.

'I tried your desk at the station,' Kat said. 'There was no answer.'

'I came home early. Are you okay?'

'Oliver's gone.'

He came alive and wiped away his tears. 'He's gone?'

'Yeah.'

'Okay. Okay. Good.'

'I'm so nervous.'

'So am I. But don't worry about a thing. I'm looking after you now. When did he leave?'

'About ten minutes ago.'

'When will he be back?'

'Not until this evening. Probably sometime after seven.'

'Okay. Get yours and the baby's things together. I'll be there in an hour. I'm already packed.'

'Really?'

'Really.'

'I don't know what to say.'

'You don't have to say anything.'

'What about your apartment?'

'I'll take care of it.'

'Okay.'

'I'll be there soon.'

'Are we doing the right thing?'

He paused. 'Of course we are. You can't go on like this. You're not safe with him, neither of you. You both deserve better.'

'You're a good man.'

He went to the bedroom and took the packed bag off the bed and set it at the front door and went out on to the balcony. He leaned on the rail and breathed. The air cold and calming. A woman was jogging along the marina. He'd seen her about. Young, about his age. Tanned and toned. Ponytail swinging. He watched her. He watched her and he pictured a life with her. House, kids, happiness, old age. Simplicity. Then she was gone and he went back inside and locked the balcony doors and pulled the blinds.

He gently strummed the strings of the guitar leaning on its stand. In the trembling decay time of the strings' sustain, a thought occurred. He took the photo of his mother and him from its frame and put it in his bag. He didn't take the graduation photo. A final look around. Wintery sunlight glancing off the marina sliced up the room through the blinds. The apartment was airless, stagnant, a dead aquarium. He saw his crucifix chain on the table by the front door and stopped to put it on and then left.

12

Orla called Liam from a payphone in a retail park indistinguishable from the many she'd driven through.

'Hello?' A woman.

'Who is this?' Orla said.

'My name's Alex.'

Liam had told Alex everything and now Alex was trying to tell Orla, to make her listen to what she had to say, but Orla yelled at her and told her to put Liam on. Alex asked if she was even aware just how badly Liam had been hurt. Orla yelled at her again. Their voices were buried in distance and then Liam came on the line.

'You told a stranger?' she said.

'After what you've put us through this week, don't dare think you can take the moral high ground here.'

'Liam, I think—'

'You're not coming home, are you?'

'Of course I am. Tonight. I need to do something first and then I'll be back.'

'What thing?'

'I'm going to sort this.'

'How?'

'I'm going to a hotel.'

'Which hotel?'

'It's called the Northern Sea. I'm on my way now. I've been an idiot but I'm going to fix things. I'm going to fix everything.'

'Orla, what are you talking about? How are you going to fix everything?'

'I'm going to leave the case in the restaurant toilets, in the ceiling. I can't think of anywhere better, not without showing ID at banks and safes. If it's in the toilets before I go to the room and anything happens to me, at least they don't get the money, you do. Get a pen, I'll give you the address.'

She read him the address Sweet had written on the business card.

'They're not getting away with what they've done to you,' she said. 'To us.'

'Just give them the money.'

'Why should I? We need it, they only want it.'

'It's a curse. You've cursed us.'

'Don't say that.'

'The moment you turned your back on those people you cursed us. You opened a door and invited evil into our lives.'

'It wasn't like that. I didn't know. I didn't know what it was, Liam.'

'But now you do,' he shouted. 'Now you do.'

When she spoke again her voice was small yet tight and controlled, precise. 'What does giving back the money achieve? They're dead. The money can't help them, but it can help us.'

'You abandoned us too.'

She pressed a fist to her forehead. 'I didn't abandon you.'

'You cursed us.'

'Stop saying that.' The receiver creaked in her grip. 'And who's that woman? Who's Alex?'

'She knocked asking for directions and we got talking.'

'You got talking.'

His tone turned to ice: 'My face is black and blue and my fucking hand is broken and she took pity on me. Is that really what you want to hear?'

A look on her face as if she'd been punched in the stomach. 'I'm sorry. I'm so sorry.'

'The baby won't stop crying, Orla. She won't stop screaming.'

'Listen, I'll be home tonight, okay? This won't take long. I promise.'

'You promise? You promise? You need to stop saying that.'

She didn't say anything else: her credit had run out.

Complete disconnection.

11

Carlin left the bank and sat in his car holding a wad of money. Another loan. He closed his bloodshot eyes. From overhead came the low rumble of a plane and he saw himself sitting there, the only passenger aboard, warm sunlight beaming in through the windows as he hurtled above clouds into another life. He looked out at the desolate street. Litter and leaves whirling about the ground. He swore repeatedly under his breath, a mantra of despair. A migraine ate through his thoughts and blood dripped from his nose. He wiped his nose on his tie and then got out and smoked a cigarette in three long drags and went into the bookie's opposite the bank.

Fluorescent tubes and tiled floors. Bolted-down metal stools and banks of TVs. A rail-thin junkie about forty wearing a track-suit sat slumped in a mobility scooter, looking up at a TV, a roll-up hanging unlit from loose, scabby lips. Carlin went to the counter, holding a ball of tissue to his nose, and handed a pre-written betting slip and the entire wad of money to the woman behind the bulletproof glass. A slight raising of her eyebrows the only indication that this was an extraordinary amount of money to put on a horse.

He sat on a stool and nursed his bloody nose and watched the race on a big TV. His vision tunnelled, his hearing jammed. He swallowed a pill. A new mantra overtook him, an incantation. *Come on come on come on.* What started as a whispered chant ended as a roaring plea. By the time the race had finished, he was on his feet. Sick and silent and pale. His horse had finished fourth.

'What can you do, eh?' The man on the mobility scooter laughed snidely. He had no teeth.

Carlin looked at the woman behind the glass. She seemed to be avoiding eye contact with him. A lean young man now stood behind her. White shirt, blue tie, gelled hair. The manager. He was looking at Carlin. Carlin looked at the TV again and scrunched up the slip and dropped it on the counter with his bloody tissue. On his way out he punched the wall so hard he fractured a bone in his wrist. He barely felt it. The manager yelled something and came out from behind the glass, following him to the door.

Carlin wheeled around and grabbed his slimy hair and dragged his head back so hard the manager almost fell to the tiles. Carlin raised his broken hand and the manager cowered. He wanted to break his nose, crack his eye socket, knock out his teeth. Instead he reached into his pocket and took out his wallet and flipped it open to display his warrant card and badge. He held it inches from the manager's face, eager to convince someone of his limited power.

Boyd's Triumph Bonneville motorbike was parked outside the alehouse when Carlin walked in. Boyd was sitting at the bar, swirling lager dregs around the bottom of a pint glass, his transfemoral prosthetic leg leaning unattached against the bar wearing a motorbike boot. Carlin ordered a pint of bitter and sat gazing at the swamped drip trays on the bar, the gleaming chrome taps, the chilled bottles in the fridges. He didn't look in the mirror behind the spirits gantry.

'Brother Carlin, as I live and breathe.' Boyd noticed Carlin's hand. 'What happened?'

Carlin looked down at his hand resting on the barrel curve of his gut. Purple and swollen, fingers hooked into a puffy claw. 'I'm finished.'

'What are you on about? Money?'

Carlin made a noise.

'How much?' Boyd said.

Carlin looked at him, deciding whether to tell him. Then did. He told him everything.

'How long have they given you?'

'Not long.'

'You must have dealt with loan sharks before.'

'As police. Not like this.'

'How's it different?'

'They send me photos.'

'Photos?'

'Surveillance photos.'

'Of what?'

'My family.' Carlin rubbed his face and groaned. 'I've got an amazing wife, daughter, granddaughter…' He trailed off, unsure where he was going with this. 'I've been so stupid.'

Boyd jiggled his empty glass at the gym-rat barman. In the grubby light they watched him angle the glass under the tap and fill it to the brim. Football news on the TV at the end of the bar. Boyd lifted his pint and knocked it against Carlin's.

'We're intelligent men. How can we make money, real money? There has to be a way.' Boyd tapped his Masonic signet ring twice on the bar. 'We're not leaving here until we think of something.'

Carlin drank his bitter and slouched on the stool. He remained in that sculpted pose of ruination a long moment. The light coming in through the textured windows glaucous and watery. He looked at his reflection behind the spirits and said: 'I'm finished.'

10

Lynch drove through the congested city in a block of spacetime carved from creation. A mute world beyond the glass streaming into the car. His hands clinging to a wheel made of air. He drove into the wealthier side of the city, and the noise and the congestion finally loosened and fell away and was replaced with trees and uncluttered roads and spaces between houses and cars. On a broad road of evergreens free of vehicles and road markings, a white L-shaped house came into view at the end of a long driveway, and the world rushed back into his skull, his senses refilling, and he surfaced from his racing thoughts.

He parked behind the soaring conifers on the front lawn and shut off the engine. Sitting in silence, he thought of nothing, he thought of everything. Possible lives stretched out of the dark and passed him by. He got out and walked to the open electric gates. The sight of Oliver's Maserati parked around the side of the house stunned him frozen. He came to and stepped back, hidden behind the trees. His skin tinted an unreal green in the leaf-strained light. He got out his phone and started dialling Kat's number and then stopped and looked up. No more hiding.

He cancelled the call and stood at the gates and looked up at the house. Then he was crossing the stone driveway, watching the windows as if expecting to see Oliver standing behind a curtain, looking back. He went around the side, carefully looking in the corners of windows. The expensively furnished interiors dark and still. He passed the Maserati and reached the kitchen door. It was open. He stopped to listen. Distant traffic, birds. No voices from inside the house.

He stepped into the kitchen and found Oliver curled in his

blood on the floor tiles. Mouth lolled, eyes half shut, skin and lips bluish grey. He leaned and felt a pulseless neck. He opened his shirt and saw the stab wound in his stomach. He straightened up and looked out through the kitchen door. A landscaped garden, tall still conifers. He passed several packed bags beside the kitchen island as he went deeper into the house.

Kat was sitting on the couch in the living room, rocking the baby. Both crying and streaked in blood. He sat and gathered them in his arms.

'He came back,' she said.

'It's okay. Don't worry.'

'What have I done?'

'It's okay. Everything's going to be okay.'

'He came back and saw my bags in the kitchen. I told him I was leaving. I told him it was over. I told him everything. He lost his mind.'

'Are you hurt? Is she hurt?'

'It's mostly his blood.'

He leaned back and studied her face. Her already bruised face puffy and wet with crying and now her nose was broken too, her mouth swollen, blood on her teeth. He pulled her into him again. Then he saw the knife on the solid oak coffee table. He leaned back and looked at her.

'Look at me. Kat, look at me. We told him we were leaving together, didn't we? We told him it was over. We said it was the end of the abuse. We said no more. Didn't we? He lost his mind and grabbed the knife.' He picked up the knife and cleaned the handle of her prints on his shirt before gripping it. 'He grabbed this knife and attacked me. I overpowered him, didn't I? It was self-defence. I overpowered him and buried this thing in him, didn't I? Didn't I? Kat, answer me. Didn't I?'

She sobbed and held his hand. 'No.'

'You were holding the baby, weren't you? You were protecting her from him, right, like you need to do right now?'

'I can't do this.'

'You can. You have to.'

'It's not fair. I won't let you.'

'You can't leave her. She can't leave you.'

'They might understand.'

'They might not. You can't risk losing her. You need each other. I'll tell them everything he ever did to you and how much you both mean to me, and they'll know I did it. There's no other way. I need to do something good, Kat. I need to do something good. The time will be easy because I was right. I'll be inside because I was right, because I did the right thing. Let me do one good thing. Please.'

He pulled them into him, held them close. They stayed that way for a long time, hugging and sniffing and wiping tears from their eyes. The colour of the day changed through the windows and he kissed their foreheads and then he broke the embrace and rose, holding the knife.

'Which hand did he use?'

She looked up at him confused.

'Was he left- or right-handed?'

Nothing.

'Kat, please, we've gotta keep it together.'

'Left. He was left-handed.'

In the kitchen he raised his right arm across his face and slashed two defence wounds in his forearm. He forced Oliver's wooden left hand to grip the knife, making sure his prints touched the handle, and then he dropped the knife to the blood-grouted tiles and fell to his knees, immersing his hands in the cold setting

174

puddle, slathering it over himself. He took Oliver's left hand by the wrist, folded the fingers into a fist and repeatedly punched it into his own face until Oliver's wedding ring split open his cheek and eyebrow. He rose and looked at his bloody face in the window. Somewhere outside, where winy light was running from the sky, a dog was barking.

9

Alex came in from the kitchen carrying a plate of buttered crackers and a cup of tea. She set the plate and the cup on the coffee table and looked down at Liam feeding the baby on the couch, eyes unfocused on the muted TV. She picked up the TV remote.

'Do you want the sound on?'

He came out of his daze. 'What?'

'Do you want the sound on?'

'No. It's just something to look at.' The baby finished feeding and looked up at him, into his eyes, and then rolled into him.

'Let me take her. You have something to eat.'

'I'm okay.'

'You should eat. Give her to me.'

She picked up the plate and set it on his lap, and he passed her the baby and sat back, taking a bite of a cracker, reflexively chewing and swallowing, jaw aching, swollen eyes back on the silent TV.

He looked at the baby in her arms. The baby looking back at him with a harried expression on her flushed, tearstained face. He set down the plate and leaned and stroked her creased forehead until it relaxed.

'What's the accent?' Liam said. 'Sounds Eastern European.'

'Where is she?'

'What?'

'Your wife. Where is she?'

He sat back. 'On her way to a hotel.'

'Which hotel?'

'She said she's going to take care of everything.'

Alex sat on the arm of the couch, bouncing the baby on her knee. 'I've been thinking. If the money's returned, whoever's after her will disappear, right? If they have their money, they've no reason to keep chasing.'

'I don't know. Maybe.'

'You'll never be safe while she has their money.'

He tried to think but his mind was in pieces, a broken mirror, reflections reflecting reflections, a loop of infinite feedback.

'You need to get the money back to these people. It's the only way they'll stop.'

'I think she's going to do something awful.'

'Then you need to save her. She can't look after her family so you need to. Act now, Liam. Correct her mistakes. She's been greedy and her greed has made her stupid. But you must remember: their greed outweighs hers.'

He touched the hot swelling around his mouth and eye with cold fingertips. The shock of the cold and the pain seemed to wake him, clear his mind, and he looked at her. This stranger he'd known a matter of hours. This stranger holding his daughter in a grip that seemed too tight. This stranger he'd invited into their home.

He said: 'How do you know their greed outweighs hers?'

8

Carlin arrived home tired and slightly drunk. He shut the front door and stood swaying in the hallway mirror. Impassive, speechless, that unshaven man in the world next door looked back with equal self-loathing. He shut his eyes and turned away and when he opened them that man was gone. But he'd be back. He always came back.

His wife was sitting on the floor in the living room among a pile of library books on genealogy. The news playing low on the TV in the background. She looked up at him and then back down and continued writing on a pad of lined paper with one of three coloured marker pens she was holding.

'You're drunk.'

He sat on the arm of the couch and watched a small fly describe a square flight path under the ceiling light.

'I've only had a few.'

'It's teatime.'

'I'm allowed to have—'

'What's wrong with your hand?'

He looked down at his inflated purple claw. 'Nothing.'

'Is it broken?'

'I said it's fine.'

'You home for the night?'

He nodded at her books. 'How's it going?'

She shut the pad and the books. 'I'll do you a coffee.'

He followed her into the kitchen, taking off his coat on the way, and sat at the table and opened the newspaper, ignoring the pile of letters and bills and credit-card junk mail. He stopped at an article buried in a corner of a page about a mass grave discovered in a mountain chain on the Romania–Serbia border. The bodies, what was left of them, estimated to have been in the ground over a year, had been sealed in Teflon-lined 55-gallon drums and dissolved with acid. The article talked of illegal immigration, organ trading, arms dealing, terrorism, human trafficking. He read the article again while the kettle boiled and then shut the paper and looked at the pile of envelopes. All addressed to him. He noticed several envelopes from the bank were open.

'I opened them.' She set a sandwich and a coffee before him on the table. 'Were you going to tell me?'

He shut his eyes but the darkness spun. He could vomit.

'I'm taking care of it.'

'How? You planning on winning the lottery? Robbing a bank? Or is the Craft going to help?' She paused. 'I thought not.'

'It's not your concern.'

She almost laughed. 'Not my concern?'

'No, it's not.'

'Is there more?'

'No.'

'You don't owe anyone else anything?'

'I said no.'

'How are we going to pay back that kind of money? With our pensions?'

He couldn't look at her, let alone tell her that the amount she'd seen in the letters was a fraction of what he owed. His phone rang in his coat pocket. She stared at him. He stared into the floor.

'You going to answer that?' she said.

He didn't say whether he would or wouldn't. Then he went into his coat and took out the phone. She lingered a moment and then went upstairs and a door shut.

He swore and answered the call.

'It's Liam, Liam McCabe, I'm in the bathroom with the baby.'

'Liam? What are you talking about? Why are you whispering?'

'There's a woman in my house. She's downstairs. I've asked her to leave but she won't go. I don't know who she is. You've got to help us.'

The baby girl bawling down the line.

'Okay, Liam, everything's fine. Speak slow and clear.'

'I invited her in but she's...I don't know who she is. She keeps talking about Orla.'

'Have you spoken to Orla?'

'She's on her way to a hotel called the Northern Sea.' He told Carlin the address and Carlin wrote it on one of the many envelopes before him on the table. 'She's going to hide the money in the restaurant toilets. Don't ask me why. Shh, it's okay, it's okay, I'm here, don't cry. Send someone to help her. I think she's going to do something stupid. Shit, she's coming.'

A low concussion down the phone.

'Liam, wait. Hello? Has she threatened you? Does she have a weapon? What's her name? Liam. Liam, speak to me.'

The line was dead. He tried calling back but the call could not be connected. He called emergency services and told the operator the situation while putting on his coat. He was about to leave when he stopped, looking at the envelope he'd written on. Plain brown with no stamp or address, just his name handwritten in red marker across the back. He tore it open.

Photos of Kat and the baby outside their home. Photos of them at the shops, in the park, filling the car at the petrol station. A photo of her walking out of a bar with Lynch and another of them huddled together under an umbrella in the rain and another of them in his car and another of them entering his apartment and

179

another of her leaving alone in a cab. He put the photos back in the envelope and folded it in half and put it inside his coat. He went to the foot of the stairs and held on to the banister. Looking upstairs, he was about to say something. Instead, he left the house dialling another number on his phone.

7

Liam picked up his phone off the bathroom floor and stepped away from the bolted door, hushing the screaming baby. He pressed his back to the furthest wall, wedging them between toilet and bath. He tried testing the phone and dropped it again. He was leaning to pick it up and struggling with his broken wrist when Alex spoke through the door.

'Liam, who were you talking to? Was it Orla? I can't help you if you won't talk to me. Liam, you're making me very nervous. Should I be worried? Are you going to do something silly?'

He reached for the window handle.

'Liam, my husband, Egan, he visited you yesterday.'

He froze.

'And I've spoken to your wife. I think she's stolen my husband's car.'

He retracted his hand and looked at the door.

'Since then, I've been unable to contact either of them. I'm afraid something's happened. All I want is you to tell me where she is. Finding her means finding my husband. I know you know. I'm just as worried as you are.'

He was reaching for the window again when something crashed against the door. And again. Another crash and the flimsy bolt pulled apart and the door swung inward and the baby somehow screamed louder than he'd ever heard. Alex stood in the doorway holding a black-bladed knife.

'If you tell me where she is, I promise that only you and her will be killed, your baby will be fine. But if you don't, if you refuse'—she pointed the knife at the weeping baby—'I'll cut off its head while you watch.'

6

Dolan stood in the doorway watching Sweet's father roll the cue ball across the snooker table and back off the cushion. The old man picked up a Scotch off the rail and drank deeply, looking at the window. Reflections of the snooker table's overhead lights stretched off into the dark vales of the hills. It wasn't until Dolan tapped on the door that the man turned and jumped back, knocking his glass over, Scotch pouring out, spreading across the green baize.

'What the fuck? Get out of my house.'

He threw the cue ball at Dolan. It slammed into his shoulder and dropped dully to the floor. Dolan moved forward and easily overpowered him, weak as he was with blanching fear. He punched the old man in the face. Slow, heavy, precise impacts, the bones of his face breaking, consciousness draining from his eyes. He fell to his knees and leaned on one hand, the other held to his face. Blood dripped through his fingers to the carpet and urine washed his trousers.

Dolan lifted the Scotch decanter to his face in a gesture of smelling and then took a sip. He walked around the desk, looking at the cigars in the Spanish cedar box and the cased pair of flintlock duelling pistols. He took out the pistols and held them and then saw his parodying reflection floating in the window out there over the hills and put the pistols back in the case. At the window he bowed into the eyepiece of the brass telescope and spied a colossal patch of space that contained nothing.

He lifted the man by his throat to his feet and walked him backward, slamming him flat on his back on to the snooker table. The old man's head smacked one of the low-hanging lights as he went down and a bulb burst, raining molten glass. The remaining lights swung shadows across the room. Dolan took out Sweet's notebook, pencil and Beretta and held them close to the man's face.

'You recognize these?'

The man's eyes floated and shut as he tried to focus.

'Your son's belongings. You sent him to kill us. We killed him.'

He penetrated the man's mouth with the Beretta, all the way to the back of his throat, teeth clinking against steel, and he looked into the man's eyes, which had regained some clarity, and the man jerked and gagged and raised his hand as if to shield himself from a light too bright or a dark too deep. Dolan pulled the trigger. A white flash in the man's mouth and nostrils, backlighting his uncomprehending eyes. The bullet punctured his throat and erupted out the back of his head, sinking through the baize into the slate of the snooker table and fracturing it. The man involuntarily bit the pistol, breaking most of his incisors, and his wasted face locked in a silent scream around the gun.

Dolan left the gun sticking out of his mouth and walked around the room, reading from Sweet's notebook and looking at the unimpressed portraits hanging from the walls. He read more of the notebook and looked at framed photos on the desk. He read, he looked. Read, looked. Sweet had seemingly annotated every observation he'd ever made. The motto under a bronze wall plaquette: *Audi. Vide. Tace.* Sweet's translation: *Hear. See. Be Silent.* Dolan tried the desk drawers. All but one opened. He looked at the man, a tremendous amount of blood glugging out the back of his head and from his ears.

He was going through the man's trouser pockets when he found a key and the key opened the locked drawer and inside the locked drawer was a series of Polaroids, sexually sadistic photos of a young woman with pink hair. Each photo more extreme, more brutal, more compromising than the last. They appeared to have been arranged chronologically over months, the pink-haired woman's abdomen steadily growing. She was pregnant. In the last photo, the woman bleary-eyed and half-naked on a wicker chair and cradling a newborn in track-marked arms, Dolan could make out in the mirror behind her that the photographer was the old man behind him.

He left the photos scattered across the desk and exited the snooker room and descended the wide carpeted steps of the central staircase. At the front door he stepped over the legs of the dead woman who'd called herself the man's wife, Sweet's mother. She lay on the stone floor, face crumpled, wig loose, one side of her bald head caved in. Sweet's phone rang in Dolan's pocket and he took it out and looked at the screen. Unknown caller. He answered but did not speak. He waited for whoever was calling to speak first.

'Is this Sweet?' A woman's voice. 'Millar Sweet?'

'Yeah.'

'It's Orla McCabe. I'll do it. I'll meet you.'

'Good.'

'Tonight, at the hotel, the Northern Sea, right?'

'Right.'

'I'll call when I'm there.' She disconnected.

Dolan spat and left the hillside manor.

5

After cleaning and redressing her wounds in the Mercedes outside the Northern Sea Hotel, Orla checked in under a false name, paid with Egan's cash and sat in the restaurant window, drinking vodka. She was so weak and disoriented from stress, blood loss, sleeplessness and too many painkillers that she felt hungover, but the drink was helping. Under the table, between her new too-small boots, stood the case.

The restaurant's interior was decorated in muted earth tones and the dim diffused lighting calmed her. Rain fell against the windows. A loose scattering of people sat about in tub chairs, eating and drinking, swiping phones, their voices murmurs. She looked at the large-screen TV showing European football and swallowed another painkiller with the vodka.

A young couple sat down at the next table and pretended not to notice the odd-looking woman with the bandage around her head and the wild eyes. He ordered an orange juice and she ordered a cappuccino. From their mannerisms it was obvious she was more into him than he was her. She leaned forward, he leaned back. She laughed, he tried to smile. They talked quietly but Orla heard enough. The young woman was leaving for a job and she asked if he'd miss her.

'Yeah,' he said.

'You're not just saying it?'

'No.'

'How much?'

'How much what?'

'How much will you miss me?'

He looked at his phone and touched the screen and then looked at her and said: 'You know, a lot.'

He took a strip of pills from his jacket pocket and popped one out and gave it to her. There was something the matter with his eyes. She swallowed the pill and then held his hand in both of hers. He picked up his phone with his free hand.

Orla sank into the chair with her vodka, watching cars and cabs pull up outside, people hauling luggage, running to avoid the rain. She remembered holding her daughter at the living-room window at three in the morning and watching rain fall like welding sparks against the amber street lights. The shape of her tiny, furled body a perfect fit in her arms. She was hug-shaped. Her emanating warmth. Her sweet milky scent. Orla finished the vodka and was about to stand when a waiter appeared and asked if she'd like a refill. She looked at the empty glass and said: 'Why not?'

She picked up the case and went to the ladies' room and entered the end cubicle and locked the door. She set the case on the cistern, sat on the toilet lid and waited for silence. Then she stepped on the lid and lifted a tile beside a light in the suspended ceiling. Dusty darkness, complex wiring, pipework. She hefted the case inside and pushed it back until only the handle was visible and then refitted the tile and stepped down and sat hunched on the toilet lid, elbows on her knees, staring at the floor. Her mind emptied out.

She took Egan's gun from her waistband and turned it over in her hands, aimed at the toilet door, squinted down its line of sight. Almost a minute passed while she tried to eject the magazine. It slid out of the handle and clattered to the floor. She picked it up and looked at the end bullet. It looked made of gold. She refitted the magazine with the dexterity of an ape. She shut her eyes and saw Egan in her home. Like a spider in a dollhouse. Her stomach tensed. She was grinding her teeth so hard they squeaked. She focused her rage on the night to come, visualizing herself standing shadowed in the hotel room, aiming at Sweet, her arm dead still and firing, firing, firing—when someone coughed.

She sat upright, staring at the partition walls, heart drumming in her chest. A cubicle door opened two away and then the door to the toilets. Sounds from the hotel rushed in like a wind. By the time she'd concealed the gun and opened the cubicle door, a woman had entered with two girls talking excitedly about the football and blocking her view of the entrance. She went back to her table.

Eyes swinging across the room. It could have been anyone. A fresh vodka stood glistening on the table. She sat and swirled the glass, rattling the ice. The young couple now sitting in silence. She still had hold of his hand in both of hers. He was still thumbing his phone. Orla sat back and looked out the windows. Rain falling hard. A bloom of indigo and a hot branch of lightning fractured the clouds, irradiating the car park in a cold, dead glare.

She went to the payphone beside the bar and held a coin in the slot but kept hold of it. Seconds stretched out. Then she let the coin fall and she dialled the number on Sweet's business card. The phone rang. And rang. Then her call was answered. No one spoke.

Orla finally said: 'Millar Sweet?'

'Yeah.'

'Room 201.'

She hung up and went back to her table. She considered calling Liam but to go through with this, she needed to remain in a vacuum and so she resisted. She would not talk to him on the phone. She would do this and then she would go home and gather him and their baby in her arms and never let them go. She looked at the football on TV. Half-time. She would go to 201 when the second half kicked off and she would turn out the lights and she would wait in the shadows for her assassin manqué and she would kill him. She would do these things and nothing would stop her.

Through the plate-glass windows, magenta lightning exposed immense waves, blazing oil platforms, a vague horizon. In a far corner of the car park, gleaming under a street light, a Jaguar parked sideways straddled two bays. She picked up the vodka and looked at the car, rain dancing on the roof, pouring down the windows. She drank and she looked at the hotel window beside her, at the glass itself, and the world outside slipped out of focus, became an intangible blur of raindrops and light and compressed depth.

Her focus readjusted when she saw in the glass the reflection of a man passing the bar. His movement odd, unsettling. Something wrong with his legs. She turned to look at him. He wore a baseball cap and a leather biker jacket and was carrying the orange case by its handle. As if sensing he was being watched, he stopped in his lurching gait and looked back across the room at her. A glass smashed behind the bar and all heads turned to look save two. He reached into his jacket and then raised his arm and pointed at her. She swallowed. A brilliant flash of white and she saw Liam and their daughter, Éabha, older and smiling and here. Then nothing. And nothing.

4

Carlin sped along the motorway in his unmarked car through a torrential downpour. Wipers on full speed, windows fogged, dash vents blowing hot air on the glass. Vehicles swung out of his way when he loomed behind them, siren howling, flashing strobes buried in the grille. He had a window down for the wind and rain to sober him up. He tried Lynch's phone but it was off. He tried his apartment and his voicemail picked up. He left a message informing him of the case's developments and told him to call back immediately. He didn't mention the surveillance photos he'd been sent. That would be a face-to-face conversation. For now, the case took precedence.

A sign for a service station appeared and he pulled in and rushed to the toilets. Prostatitis playing havoc with his plumbing. After standing far too long at the urinal and in sweat-inducing pain, he splashed his face with cold water, swallowed painkillers and bought a first-aid kit from a shop in the concourse, quickly smoking a cigarette as he rushed back to his car through the rain. He was recklessly merging back into the motorway while wrapping a bandage around his aching and discoloured hand when a call came in on the radio. He picked up and a man said over background traffic: 'We got it.'

In the windowless security suite of the Northern Sea, Carlin and three detectives stood drinking coffee and watching silent surveillance video of the hotel restaurant.

From a high corner angle Orla McCabe sits at a window table, drinking, watching the world go by, a bandage wrapped around her head and under her jaw as if she'd had a facelift. A young couple sitting beside her holding hands. After speaking with a waiter, Orla walks out of frame carrying an orange case lifted from under her table. Three minutes later, the waiter clears her table and sets down a fresh vodka. Six minutes pass before Orla returns to the table, empty-handed. She drinks the vodka and looks relaxed, unconcerned. Rain and lightning in the windows. She uses the payphone. She sits back down and looks out the window. Some four minutes later a man enters the frame in the top corner and lurches directly to the toilets. He wears a baseball cap and a leather biker jacket and his limp is pronounced. She seems not to notice him. He emerges from the ladies' room two minutes later, carrying the orange case. And now she notices him. She turns from the window and looks at him. He looks back. Then, inexplicably, he draws a pistol from his jacket, aims at her and fires. Six mute muzzle flashes. The vodka glass explodes in her hand and her entire front turns red. The windows behind her are blown out, showering her and the nearby couple. Seats, tables and floor instantly covered in blood and broken glass. Next frame she's slumped under the table. The young man is spread over his table with the side of his neck ripped apart. The young woman with him crawls backward up her seat trying to flee the horror. Carrying the orange case, the shooter exits the frame in the same lurching manner he entered it. The young woman wanders off, stunned, arms held out like a sleepwalker. The frame remains static but for rain and lightning coming in through the blown-out windows and the pooling red that slowly rings the dead like holes to Hell opening beneath them.

The tape was paused and the four detectives stepped back from the monitor.

'Paramedics arrived seven minutes later. Both pronounced dead at the scene.'

The door to the security suite opened and the hotel manager entered, accompanied by a young man in a uniform carrying a tray of sandwiches, cakes, biscuits, coffee.

'Some refreshments,' the manager said.

The young man set down the tray and the manager looked expectantly at the detectives. 'Can I get you anything else?'

They said no and she and the young man left.

Three of the detectives helped themselves.

'Not hungry?'

Carlin looked at the tray. 'No.'

'The family has been contacted for the man, not for the woman. Didn't have any ID on her. Reception said she checked into 201 under the name'—looking in his notebook—'Hobbs, uh, Mildred Hobbs. Paid in cash. She was carrying a loaded pistol—a Glock—and missing an ear, hence the bandage.'

'Christ.'

'Tell them about the cuffs.'

Carlin's phone rang in his pocket and the detectives looked at him. He took out the phone and looked at the caller ID. Kat. He cancelled the call and sent her a text—*Busy call u soon x*—and switched off the phone.

'Besides the hand cannon, the missing ear and the mystery case—'

'And the bite mark on her thigh.'

'And the bite mark on her thigh, besides all that, paramedics said they found cuff bracelets with cut links around her wrists and ankles.'

'What the fuck?'

'Whoever she was, she was in deep.'

'Her name's Orla McCabe.'

The detectives looked at Carlin.

'You know her?'

'Been looking for her for the past week.'

'What's her story?'

'Doesn't really have one. She just stepped in some dogshit and has been leaving a mess everywhere she's gone since.'

'Well, someone needs to contact her family. Does she have anyone?'

Carlin sighed. 'She does. A husband and baby. I'll do it.'

'One more thing. Van Gogh had a card on her.'

'What kind of card?' Carlin said.

'Like a business card.'

'What kind of business?'

'That's the thing. The card was blank except for a phone number and the hotel's address handwritten on it. We're assuming that's who she was calling on the payphone.'

'You rang it?' Carlin said.

'Nothing. It's dead.'

After a brief silence, the fourth detective who was yet to speak gestured to Carlin's bound hand. 'How goes it, Brother Carlin?'

Carlin went slowly down the corridor to the restaurant entrance. Forensics and police and paramedics. Camera flashes. Clusters of staff. People streaming all around, some ducking under police tape, some recording on phones. He looked through the movement and saw the bodies under the sheets. Broken glass and blood everywhere. On a wall in the restaurant was a sign pointing to the toilets.

He moved through the crowded lobby and out of the hotel into the night storm. The impact of the rain forming glassy domes that slid adrift across the surfaces of puddles. He got in his car and sat there recalling nights lying in bed beside his sleeping wife, imagining her life without him, how she and Kat would cope with his suicide. He guessed after the initial shock they'd be okay and better off with him out of the way.

He picked up the radio and made a call. It was answered immediately.

'What the fuck, Boyd? I never said kill anyone. I said get the money and run.'

'Fuck her. She shouldn't have reached for a gun.'

'I saw the footage. She didn't reach for a fucking gun and you know it.' He wiped his steamed window and looked at the sea, black and fearsome through the trees. 'I'm finished.'

He didn't notice the yellow Saleen Mustang pull up behind him without its headlights on.

3

Without warning the first armed response vehicle appeared in the dead-end street outside the McCabes' terraced home. No lights, no sirens. Four armed officers filed out. Two went around the back and two went to the partially open front door. They made hand gestures and then pushed it open and stepped inside and moved upstairs, rifle stocks pressed into their shoulders. At the top of the stairs all doors were shut but for the bathroom. It had been forced open, door and jamb split at the edges. One officer made a hand gesture and then pushed open the door and the other officer moved in, rifle first. Liam McCabe lay in his blood on the linoleum, wearing a shirt sling, his face a beaten ruin, his head wedged at a horrible angle under the toilet. Beside him lay his daughter. Slathered and rolled in her father's blood, she looked larval. His arm lay across her, pinning her to the floor, and she gazed about, hands squeezing, chubby legs slowly pedalling the air, ominously mute. She was dredged from the cold setting blood and taken to the landing and checked for wounds. Save the bruises on her forehead and arms, as if she'd been tightly gripped, she was unharmed. The officer called it in while the officer crouching beside Liam removed a glove and felt his throat. As far as she could tell, he'd been stabbed at least six times in the chest and stomach. She hung her head and shut her eyes. Through the fern-frosted window a helicopter drifted beneath its pounding blades, searchlight swinging through the dark. Then she felt it: a slow and distant pulse.

2

The following night Dolan materialized from a dark grove of trees carrying a splitting maul. He crossed a long dirt path towards a mansion surrounded by the jagged black cut-outs of hills, a modern glass box that cast a warm glow across the dark waters of a lake. In the carport on the block-paving driveway sat a horse trailer and a car cloaked in a grey waterproof cover. He stood balanced on the rear tyre of the trailer and looked in through the wired glass. An old Triumph Bonneville motorbike lay inside on the floor. He pulled off the car cover and looked through the dark windows of a yellow Saleen Mustang and saw a dash-mounted police computer and radio.

Light from the mansion's floor-to-ceiling windows lay moated across the aluminium decking that bordered the house. He passed under the security light fitted over the front doors and the shadow of his hood scrolled down his face. He circled the house. Lakeside stood a shirtless and stocky man leaning on the deck rail, looking out into the water. His flesh was covered in dark licks of blood and it steamed in the cold. Hearing footsteps, he turned. An expressionless face gave way to paling fear at the sight of the hooded and malformed figure carrying a splitting maul. He contracted and backed up into the house, palms raised.

Dolan stalked him through sliding glass doors into an extensive living area where a canvas oil painting of a Dobermann spanned an entire wall. When the man turned to run, Dolan buried the axe side of the splitting maul in the back of his head. He was dead before he hit the floor. Dolan set his boot on the handprint tattoo inked between the scapulae and levered free the maul. He listened. Nothing but the low rumble of a fire recessed in a rectangular hole in a wall. He moved deep into the house.

Along a spotlit hallway of bare white walls, he came to a door that opened into a low-lit office. A flawlessly dressed woman of about fifty sat smoking a joint behind a large steel desk bare save for an ashtray, a glass of red wine and a bulky orange case. He entered the office and the woman saw him and stood up.

Raw-boned and noseless, he looked more skull than face. She paled and tried to speak but the words came apart in her mouth.

At the far end of the room a naked grey-headed man sat in a wooden armchair on a sheet of plastic. Head hung, chin resting on breastbone, body marbled with blood. Nails had been driven through his wrists into the chair arms and through his feet into the floorboards. Wires linked to a truck battery had been fed into slashes in his legs and armpits, his neck, down the length of his penis. He was lit by a TV hooked up to a camcorder. The TV angled for his eyes only.

'Henry.' The woman directed her calls at the door behind Dolan. 'Henry.'

'He's not coming.'

'You, get the fuck out of my house. Now.'

She called for Henry again as she quailed into the corner behind the desk. He set the splitting maul on the desk beside the case and moved towards her, taking one of her fending hands by the wrist and holding it to his heart, making her feel its slow thump. She turned her head to his leaning face. He made a sound like sniffing, taking in her scent through the black teardrop eaten through the middle of his face. He ran his eyes down hers as he put her under.

He crossed the room to the body slumped in the chair and looked at the TV. An image paused on the screen of another man chained to a white plastic shower chair. Naked but for stainless-steel dog tags on a chain about his neck and the blood-splashed pet-cone that hid his entire head. On the floor beside him lay his amputated leg flensed to the bone. It took Dolan a moment to realize that the leg was in fact prosthetic.

He went through the piled clothes that had been scissored off the body of the grey-headed man and found a leather wallet.

He opened it. A police warrant card. Detective Chief Inspector Carlin. He lifted the head of the sitting corpse and compared its face to the photo. Same man. He looked at the metal badge, touched it, pocketed it. Back at the desk he opened the orange case and looked at the money.

1

In later months Lynch sat on the edge of his bed in the concrete tomb of his single cell. Single for his protection. They still got to him. He looked through beaten eyes at the photo of his mother and him, remembering the time she'd held him in her arms in the small back room of their old house and how together they'd watched snow flow silently out of the night. His earliest memory. Lifetimes ago. He put the photo in its envelope and slid it under his pillow with the letters from friends on the force and from Kat. He pulsed with a motherless ache.

According to the newspapers, which he'd followed obsessively since his incarceration, Carlin was last seen leaving the Northern Sea Hotel on the night Lynch was in an interrogation room confessing to Oliver's manslaughter. Motorway surveillance cameras picked up Carlin's car several times but lost track somewhere near the north-east coastline around midnight, the same time its GPS fleet-tracker ceased broadcasting. His car was later found torched under a pier, minus a body. His wife talked of his depression and massive debt problems he'd hidden from her, leading police to suspect suicide by drowning. Lynch had suspected they were right. But why torch the car? The answer came three days later when Carlin's tortured body was discovered in a lakeside mansion, along with the bodies of his apparent abductors and torturers, the wife and son of the murdered Cyrus Green. The son, Henry, the monster with the handprint tattoo from the videos. Cyrus Green's wife was also the sister of the pharmaceutics CEO who'd been found murdered along with his wife at their opulent home. Explicit photos of the pregnant pink-haired woman from the moors found scattered on the CEO's desk. Their son, Millar Sweet, identified as one of the bodies found on that trembling farmstead east of Eden that Lynch had visited with Carlin in a past life. The identity of the castrated giant buried inverted remained unknown. How the McCabes had become involved in this havoc Lynch never fully understood, and since he'd recovered from his attack, Liam McCabe had said nothing. Lynch didn't blame him. He'd lost his wife and uncle and suffered life-changing injuries and now had to raise his daughter alone. Some things are best left buried.

Echoic shouting and slamming doors in that mausoleum of live burials. The cell a dead womb, the prison a dead mother, he the limbo-dwelling stillborn. He gazed into the scuffed floor for what may have been seconds or hours. The clock was frozen in there. He looked up at the window overlooking the yard where snow fell down the night and down his beaten eyes.

The door hatch opened and eyes looked in and the hatch closed and the door opened. A prison officer stepped inside carrying a paper bag. He looked both ways before closing and relocking the door.

'How's it going, lad?' the officer said.

'Not bad, mate. What are you doing here? Thought we weren't playing till Wednesday.'

The officer sat down at the small metal desk. On the desk sat a fan, a phone and charger, a pack of cards, a Bible, a PlayStation and a TV draped with coloured Christmas lights.

'Just thought I'd come say hello,' the officer said.

He took a bottle of whisky from the paper bag, already opened, some of it missing, and took a swig and handed it to Lynch. Lynch took two cups from under his bed and set them on the mattress and filled both.

'You better not be driving,' he said.

'Amy's picking me up.' The officer switched on the TV and lowered the volume and picked up the cards, shuffled, dealt. He looked at Lynch's battered face and sighed, shaking his head. 'Just give me their names, lad.'

'I'll take care of it.'

The officer stopped dealing and looked at him. 'When? After they've broken your nose again. After they've blinded you. You're police inside, lad. They'll never leave you alone. Just give me their names and they'll never touch you again. I'll make sure they're tube-fed and pissing blood for the next six months. Not a problem.'

'I said I'll take care of it.' Lynch paused. 'Listen, I'm sorry, mate. I appreciate everything you've done. All this.' He gestured to the contents of the desk and the whisky. 'I really do, more than you could know, but this is something you can't help me with. This is something I've got to do on my own.'

They played poker and drank. A spaghetti western on the TV in the background.

'I haven't seen Paddy in a while,' Lynch said.

The officer sipped from his cup and looked at his cards. 'You're not going to.'

'What are you talking about?'

'He's gone.'

'What do you mean, gone? Like a transfer?' Lynch studied him.

The officer picked up another card. He looked down when he saw Lynch watching him. 'I'm going as well.'

'What?'

'I'm done. I'm finished here.'

'You're leaving?'

'Tonight.'

'Tonight? What's going on?'

The officer went quiet again.

'The suspense is killing me,' Lynch said.

The officer brought the cup to his lips and spoke into it, his entombed voice small and empty. 'It's complicated.' He drank. Then he said: 'I can't say.'

'You can't say? You and Paddy have been like brothers to me in here and you can't tell me why you're leaving? The shit I've told you. Shit I've never told anyone.' Lynch sat back, looking at him. 'And in case you hadn't noticed, I'm not police any more.'

The officer wiped his mouth and set his cards down on the desk. He couldn't look at Lynch.

'You know what, forget it,' Lynch said. 'None of my business. Sorry for prying.'

The officer looked up slowly. 'Listen, not a word of this to anyone, okay?'

'Of course.'

'I mean it, lad.'

'So do I.'

The officer opened the door and checked outside and then locked it and poured more whisky into his cup.

'A while back, Paddy got wind from some loudmouth pikey in here about a deal going down at some rich prick's shooting box on the moor. We didn't know what kind of deal, just assumed it was drugs or something. Didn't matter. What mattered was the money. This pikey, he didn't know exactly how much, but said he'd heard it was enough fuck-you money to disappear for ever. That night over a few jars, me and Paddy, we thought, you know what, we're not getting any younger, and while we're working here as wage-slaves, we'll never have any of the finer things in life. Day after day in this fucking hole surrounded by scum. This looked like a way out. No offence.'

Lynch said nothing.

'Anyway, we decided to hit this place, hard. We were going to walk right in, guns blazing, and take whatever the fuck we wanted. I mean, it wasn't a bank, no ordinary people. Who gives a shit? We studied the land and the roads, the sunset times, the weather. Everything. We even went hiking round there to get used to the terrain. That night we waited about a hundred yards back behind some rocks and then sat there watching all these shit-hot cars and bikes pulling up. Then this flatbed truck appeared loaded with big steel oil drums.'

'What was in them?'

'Fuck knows. Everything was unloaded around the back. Anyway, once everyone's inside, we're putting on gloves and ski masks and loading these sweet Remi shotguns Paddy's brother got us, when we hear shooting. We look up and this fella's standing in the doorway just unloading on some pink-haired woman who's running out into the moor. Then he goes back inside, cool as fuck.'

'What happened to the woman?' Blood had drained from Lynch's face and pooled heavily, revoltingly in his stomach. 'Did you ever find out?'

'No idea. She just limped off into the dark.' The officer lowered his eyes and sipped his whisky. 'Anyway, next thing, war breaks out inside. Lights flashing in the windows. Fucking bang, bang,

bang. Nonstop. About a minute later when everything's calmed down, we see this same fella come staggering out carrying this bright orange case. He's reeling towards the cars parked around the side, his legs going from under him, and he's about to get in one of the Audis when he falls flat on his face, dead.

'We give it a few minutes, just sit there, both in shock, like. Then we head over and look through the windows into the living room. It's like the Wild fucking West in there. Blood, guns, bodies everywhere. We go over to the fella in the gravel, careful he's not still kicking, and we open the case and look inside…and there's the money. Right there. Paddy stabs the tyres and we take the money and run. Never had to fire a bullet.' He looked at the cards in his hands and then looked at Lynch. 'We would have.'

The spaghetti western had reached its cemetery stand-off and outside the world had frozen solid. A blank and lifeless orb.

'Easy as that,' Lynch said.

'Easy as that.'

'You take the money and run.'

'We take the money and run.' The officer smiled. 'But that's not the best part.'

'No?'

'The best part is what we did in the months leading up to the deal.'

Lynch arched his eyebrows. 'Which was?'

'I knew a fella who'd done time in here about four years ago. Me and Paddy found him living in a hovel down south and we went along for a wee chat. He was cagey but desperate and we said we'd cut him in. We asked how long it'd take him to print a block of money. He asked how much. We said it didn't matter, just enough to fill a gym bag. That was when he admitted he'd carried on printing the minute he was released. He got us what we needed and that night we took it with us to the moor. While Paddy was stabbing the tyres, I swapped the real money in the case for the counterfeit money in the gym bag.'

'Why leave fake money?' Lynch said.

'So the police find a pile of money and don't suspect any missing. If they have the money, then they're not looking, and if they're not looking, then we're safe.'

'But the money was fake.'

'Even better. Makes them think the deal went south because one group was trying to fuck the other group with fake cash. Turns out they fucked each other without our help. Over what? Who knows? And that's still not the best part.'

Lynch waited.

'The fake money, it was all fifties in pounds sterling. The money we took, the money from the case, the real money, it was all in euros…in five-hundreds.' He shook his head, laughing to himself.

Lynch rubbed his knuckles across his mouth. 'Did you ever find out what the deal was for?'

'We heard something about, I don't know, human trafficking, something like that.' He shook out whisky dregs from his cup and sat back, his smile gone. 'How were we to know?'

'You don't worry what you do in the dark will be brought to the light?'

'Look out the window. The dark between the stars is vast and getting vaster. Light is a myth.'

The door hatch opened and the officer raised a hand without looking and the hatch closed.

'You carried on working so it didn't look odd, you and Paddy just walking out at the same time,' Lynch said.

'Exactamundo.'

'So, what now?'

'I work till the morning and then I'm gone.' He looked at his watch. 'Anyway, just thought we'd have one last drink. Give me a bell when you get out, I'll make sure you're taken care of. Merry Christmas, lad.' He knocked their cups together. 'See you on the other side.'

Before locking the door between them, the officer said something else, something about evil, but Lynch couldn't hear. His world had stopped spinning. He sat alone in that timeless purgatory, crucifix in fist, watching snow flow silently out of the night.

0

Perfect dark. Then windscreen wipers clearing an arc through snow and morning light entering white and brittle. The driver's breathing was laboured, his profile horribly deformed. Before him on the dashboard lay the detective's warrant card. He held the steering wheel with both hands and looked out across the road at the high perimeter wall and the staff car park. Soon prison officers were filing out through full-height turnstiles and into the flurrying dawn snow. He focused on a specific officer accompanied by three others. They smoked and talked and then hugged and shook hands and parted ways. The officer got in a red BMW driven by a woman and the car pulled out into the road. Tail lights glowing pink on the whitened ground. He started the engine and followed.

AVAILABLE AND COMING SOON
FROM PUSHKIN VERTIGO

Jonathan Ames

You Were Never Really Here

A Man Named Doll

Olivier Barde-Cabuçon

*The Inspector of Strange and
Unexplained Deaths*

Sarah Blau

The Others

Maxine Mei-Fung Chung

The Eighth Girl

Amy Suiter Clarke

Girl, 11

Candas Jane Dorsey

The Adventures of Isabel

Martin Holmén

Clinch

Down for the Count

Slugger

Elizabeth Little

Pretty as a Picture

Louise Mey

The Second Woman

Joyce Carol Oates (ed.)

Cutting Edge

John Kåre Raake

The Ice

RV Raman

A Will to Kill

Tiffany Tsao

The Majesties

John Vercher

Three-Fifths

Emma Viskic

Resurrection Bay

And Fire Came Down

Darkness for Light

Those Who Perish

Yulia Yakovleva

Punishment of a Hunter